Fuel Fire and Freedom

A Collection of Outlaw Biker Stories

Alex McRae

Published by Iron Battalion Press

Made in the USA

2025

Visit Alex McRae at www.alexmcrae.net to sign up to the author's newsletter and learn more about Iron Battalion books.

Twitter : @AlexMcRae99

Instagram: @alexmcrae99

Amazon :
https://www.amazon.com/stores/AlexMcRae/author/B0F344WTHB

Contents

Desert Blood, City Smoke

Harlan "Grinder" Voss had chewed through half the state of Arizona when it came to women. Bartenders, waitresses, single moms, and even a rodeo queen, once. Every one of them ended the same, screaming matches, lies, or walking out the door with his leather jacket still hanging off their shoulders.

One night in a Nogales dive, he slammed down his beer and spat, "I'm done with Arizona women. Nothin' but rattlesnakes in boots."

The next week, he was on a plane to New York City, his Harley shipped ahead. The boys in his club thought he'd lost his damn mind. But Grinder figured if he couldn't find a wife in the desert, maybe the city would cough up something better.

At first, it was thrilling. Neon streets, women in high heels, accents sharp as broken glass. He dated artists, fashion PR girls, and one lawyer who liked his scars more than his stories. They called him "exotic," a desert outlaw with dust in his beard and murder in his eyes.

But it didn't take long for the shine to wear off.

The women he met were cold and calculating. They liked him for the novelty, for the danger he carried in his shoulders, but none of them wanted the man who spent nights fixing an old Panhead in the garage or sitting quietly under desert stars. In New York, he was a toy. In Arizona, at least he was a man.

One night, he rode his Harley across the Brooklyn Bridge, headlights painting the river gold. The city howled around him, sirens and horns, but all he could think about was the smell of mesquite, the way Arizona women cursed like they meant it, the wild laugh of a girl who could down whiskey straight and still dance barefoot in the dust.

He realized then that he didn't hate Arizona women. He hated what he'd turned them into in his head. They were tough, fiery, and raw. They didn't fake smiles or ask what brand his boots were. They gave as good as they got.

The next morning, Grinder grabbed his gear and rode his Harley back west.

When his boots hit desert dirt again, he felt the truth settle in his bones. He wasn't made for skyscrapers or polished accents. He was made for Arizona, dust, fire, and women who could break him in half if he wasn't careful.

That night, back at the club's bar, one of the old flames he swore off walked in, still mean, still gorgeous, still Arizona through and through. She glared at him across the room.

And for the first time in months, Harlan Voss smiled.

The Curse of the Iron Rider

Chapter One

Steve cruised past the Van Buren, a downtown Phoenix rock club where he sometimes bartended. No gigs tonight, so it was deserted. He was just turning left onto 3rd Avenue when a drunk, stumbling Native American Indian stepped right in front of him. He slammed on his brakes, nearly dropping his bike. Everyone drops their bike at least once in their riding life, but Steve hadn't done it in a good ten years and wasn't planning to anytime soon. He loved his Dyna Wide Glide. It was like an extension of himself, so finely tuned and by far his favorite bike of any he had ever owned.

He was so pissed off that he cursed out the old drunk.

"You stupid bastard, I have the right of way!" he shouted.

Instead of scurrying out of the road, the old man turned and faced Steve. He pulled out a long bone (or was it a stick of petrified wood?) and started ranting at him. Steve couldn't figure out what he was saying, but he could tell from the tone that it wasn't anything nice.

"Get out of the fucking road, asshole!" he screamed at the geezer before swerving past him and heading up 3rd Ave.

"Geez, even as little kids, we knew not to stand in the middle of the road," Steve swore under his breath. He wasn't sure why he let the old fart get to him, but he was still seething a block later when he pulled up to his friend's place.

Mike was a good buddy. He and Steve had known each other for a few years now and tried to hang out at least once a week. Because

Mike lived in downtown Phoenix, it was a lot easier to drop in and see him when Steve was in the city, versus Mike visiting him at his house in Anthem, which was the last suburb on the way out of town when you were heading north.

The added benefit of visiting Mike at his place was that he had a driveway, so Steve didn't have to park his beloved Harley on the street. While downtown was gentrifying rapidly, there were still cases of meth zombies every now and then. Nobody wanted one of them messing with their motorcycle.

Mike and Steve had a couple of beers and watched some TV, shooting the shit and catching up since they last saw each other. After two beers, Steve decided it was time to leave. If he stayed any longer, he knew damn well he would be drinking all night and crashing on Mike's couch. A time came during every drinking session when you had to tap out or commit to not stopping. That time was now.

Steve straddled his Harley and fired up his trusted machine. He sat there for a moment, just listening to his engine idling away. There was a sense of rhythm, almost a musicality to it. If you didn't ride, you would not understand.

He kicked his scooter into gear and rolled out of Mike's driveway and onto 3rd Avenue. The coast was clear. He planned to find the freeway on-ramp, ride the I-10 westbound, and then at the Stack grab the I-17 north (Black Canyon Freeway) home toward Anthem.

Steve got onto the I-10 Freeway west with ease. His bike was perfectly tuned. Who needed an onboard music system when your motorcycle made such a beautiful noise on its own?

Traffic was fairly light. The I-10 was a weird freeway. It could be congested at, say, 10 a.m. on a Wednesday morning and free-flowing on a busy Saturday night. You could never tell. Just toss a coin and take a guess was the general rule. Tonight, traffic was moving with no delays, so Steve was happy.

As Steve got closer to the exit for the freeway north, he swung into the right-hand lane. He cruised over so smoothly it felt like he was surfing. There was no other feeling like it.

As Steve was getting ready to take his exit, something weird happened. He couldn't go right. It was like his handlebars were locked. He tried leaning. He tried counter-steering. Nothing. It was like his bike had a mind of its own. Panicked, he tried blipping down the gears. No luck. In fact, his bike started speeding up. What was going on? This had never happened before.

To make matters even worse, he was spotted by a cop cruising the right-hand lane. He missed his turnoff, and now he was speeding past law enforcement. Not cool. At first, Steve thought he might have gotten away with it, but no such luck. They must have been waiting for their onboard radar to calculate his speed. Red and blue lights flickered in his rearview mirror.

Well, I can't slow down. Maybe I can outrun them, Steve figured.

He flicked his right wrist, twisting his throttle. Just for a moment, he sped up, then, to his horror, he was losing power. No matter how hard he twisted his throttle, his bike was betraying him and slowing down. What on earth? Had his clutch slipped? Nope, he was in top gear. This was nuts. First, he couldn't slow down; now, he couldn't speed up. This had never happened before. He would have to give his precious Dyna a full overhaul when he got home tonight.

He was losing speed, and the cop was gaining. What could he do? He couldn't pull over; his handlebars wouldn't turn. Just as he thought that, his bike started veering to the right. "Oh, now you work, you fuckers?" Steve was furious at his trusted Harley. In all the years of ownership, it had never let him down. "Now this happens tonight?" he was enraged.

The cop was actually a decent dude. Steve lied and said his clutch was slipping, and the guy gave him a basic speeding ticket. He could argue it in court, but he resigned himself to just paying it online the next morning. Not worth the hassle.

Once the cop let him go, he continued heading west until he spied an exit ramp. He took that, got back on the I-10 eastbound, and rode back toward the Stack, where he could join the freeway north. "Oh, so now his bike was handling well? What the heck?" he muttered.

Regardless, Steve was too tired to do anything about it tonight. He would spend tomorrow morning pulling his bike apart and finding out what exactly was wrong with the old girl.

Chapter Two

Steve slept like shit that night. Strange, weird dreams. He dreamt he was in some underground tunnel system, like a series of survivalist underground bunkers or something. Was he foreseeing the future? He hated to say it, but his brain told him it was the very distant past. How could this be? He woke up shaking and in a pool of sweat. What the hell? He hadn't had nightmares since he was about twelve years old.

Steve got up, took a piss, and headed to his kitchen to make some coffee. Without his morning coffee, he could never get his brain in gear. As he sat and listened to the pot percolate, his phone went off. He contemplated letting it go to voicemail. Way too early to actually speak to someone. Usually, if someone rang him, he would wait to see if they followed up with a text. Why take a call when you can just read a text? Chances are it wasn't that urgent, whatever the person was calling about.

Steve looked at his phone. It was his buddy Mike. Why was he calling? Did he leave his riding gloves at Mike's last night? Nope, there they were on his kitchen countertop. Oh, fuck it, curiosity got the better of him. He decided to take the call.

"Hello?" he answered.

"Hey, it's me," said Mike.

"Yeah, I know, it comes up on screen," Steve explained.

"Ah, yeah, duh," Mike replied. "Did you hear about Brian?"

"No. What about Brian?" asked Steve.

"He's dead," said Mike.

That woke Steve up. No caffeine needed.

"Wait, what?" asked Steve. Anyone who knew Brian knew he was the most cautious rider ever in the Steel Reapers Motorcycle Club.

"He's dead, man. Riding to work this morning," said Mike.

"Ugh. Let me guess. Drunk driver?" asked Steve. "No, some chick texting, right?"

"Actually, no. He ran a red light, doing ninety in a forty-mile-an-hour zone," said Mike.

"Brian? Our Brian? The most cautious rider in the entire club? Ain't no way," said Steve. "No way at all."

"I'm telling you the truth, bro. He's dead," said Mike.

"Look, I believe you. No one is calling you a liar. I just can't see Brian doing that. The cops must have got it wrong," Steve replied.

"I know what you're saying," said Mike, "but it's true. It's all true."

"Damn. Mike, look, I believe ya. I just woke up. Let me drink my coffee and call you back. I need time to come to grips with this."

"Okay, man. I'll be around. Gimme a call back when ya can," said Mike.

"I will," said Steve. "Oh, and thanks for calling, man. Appreciated."

"Anytime, man," said Mike.

"Oh," said Steve. "Be safe out there, okay?"

"I will, bro. I will," said Mike before hanging up.

Steve spent the rest of the morning working on his bike. He pulled pretty much everything apart and back together again and could find nothing wrong with it. After putting it all back together, he let it sit idling on his garage floor, listening to the engine chugging away. It sounded like music to his ears. A perfectly tuned machine. He was happy.

After lunch, he decided to go for a power nap. He had a terrible headache, and he never got headaches. Once again, he had strange dreams. This time, he was somewhere in Northern Arizona, walking barefoot through a canyon. Where were his boots? He had no clue.

Yet again, he awoke in a cold sweat. His phone was ringing. He grabbed it. Mike again? What now?

"Hello?" he answered groggily.

"Steve, it's Mike," said Mike.

"I know," said Steve. "What's up?"

"So, check this out," said Mike. "Tucson Tim went to the police station. They showed him security camera footage."

"Okay…" said Steve, waiting for Mike to finish the story.

"Sure enough, Brian was speeding," said Mike, "and he wasn't wearing his helmet!"

Now, Arizona was a state where it was legal to ride without a helmet; the choice was yours. However, Brian was a guy who would rock a full-face helmet even if he was just going to ride around the block. When he had first been patched into the club, one of the older guys had had a bad crash and slid face-first down the freeway, leaving him with a bad eye and horrific facial scars. That was more than enough to convince Brian to always wear a full-face helmet. What was he thinking?

"Wow! That's weird," said Steve.

"No! Not even," said Mike. "It gets weirder."

Weirder? Steve doubted it. Nothing was weirder than Brian speeding and not wearing a helmet.

"Go on," said Steve.

"He called me from the central cop station to tell me this," explained Mike.

"Okay."

"So, about four hours later, I get a call from Tucson Tim's old lady," said Mike.

"Is she okay?" asked Steve.

"Yeah, she's fine. But Tim got hit by a big rig on the 202 Freeway on his way back from the police station."

"Huh? What are you telling me?" asked Steve.

"Tim's dead, bro. He died."

Steve felt like he was about to pass out. He felt dizzy. He felt sick. "Tim's dead?"

"Yes. He died instantly," said Mike solemnly.

"Dude, what the fuck is going on?" asked Steve.

"I dunno, man. I dunno," said Mike.

The pair chatted a little longer, then Steve realized it was time to go to work. Tonight, he was bartending at a local sports bar in Anthem, a quick five-minute ride from his house. The atmosphere sucked, but the regulars usually tipped pretty well.

He showered and got dressed. He grabbed his riding gear and went to start his bike. He turned the ignition, and nothing. Are you kidding me? thought Steve. I had spent all morning working on her, and she was running great. What the heck?

He had no time to take her back apart and troubleshoot. He had to leave for work. He grabbed his phone and ordered an Uber. One of the female bartenders could give him a lift home at the end of the night. The bar was local but just far enough that walking was impractical. He had to get a ride in.

Chapter Three

The local sports bar was actually busy midweek for a change. Steve didn't get home until a little past 3 a.m. On a whim, he decided to check on his bike even though he was a little buzzed and a lot tired. He entered his garage and went to start her up. Hey presto, what do you know? She started on the first try. What the heck?

He was too tired to have another go at stripping her down. He would have to leave that until tomorrow.

Steve showered and crashed out in a haze of drunkenness and exhaustion. Even then, he didn't sleep well. He had terrifying visions of ancient spirits and vivid dreams of graphic bike crashes. Once again, he woke up drenched in sweat with his heart pounding. What the hell? Seriously, he hadn't had nightmares like this since he was a kid. He got up and made his way to the kitchen to brew some coffee.

As he sat alone in his kitchen, he started thinking about that old Indian man he had shouted at back on Van Buren. Was he a Hopi medicine man or something? Had he cursed him? When he was younger, he was taught that ancient curses, whether Gypsy, Wiccan, or Native American, were nothing more than the power of suggestion. You think you are under a curse? Then you will be under one. You don't think you are under a curse? Then it won't affect you. Steve was starting to think this might be a gross oversimplification. If he had been cursed, what could he do to lift it?

He thought back to that goth girl he dated after his divorce. Stefani? Did he still have her number? She was into all that chakra, aura, and spell stuff. She could probably help him. He would drink his morning coffee and give her a call.

Stefani came over that afternoon with a case filled with herbs and incense. She told him to leave her alone in his garage as she performed her "exorcising" ritual.

Stefani came back into Steve's kitchen about 90 minutes later. Steve noticed that his garage now smelled like some exotic incense.

"It's all done," Stefani proudly announced.

Steve offered her money for her services, but she refused. They both sat and had a beer and caught up before she left. Pleased that she had done her job, Steve grabbed his riding gear to go for a test run.

Sure enough, once in his garage, despite the stench of Nag Champa incense, his Harley started up right away. Good ol' Stefani. Why did he ever break up with her?

He kicked his scoot into gear and rolled out of his garage. He wasn't going to go far, just around the neighborhood. Steve went down to the end of his road, took a left, and kicked up into second gear. Everything felt good, just like it always did. He shifted into third and built up speed. In two blocks, he would have to slow down to turn right and start making his way toward his home.

As he got closer to the corner, he eased off on the throttle, but the bike didn't slow down. In fact, he started gaining speed. He tried downshifting, but nothing worked. His precious Harley was worse than ever. Stupid Stefani had done nothing but waste his time! He was approaching the turn with way too much speed, 75 mph now.

He gave a silent prayer to the motorcycle gods that there was no oncoming traffic. He counter-steered and noted that, at least this time, his handlebars were not locking up. Steve went into the turn knowing he was already traveling way too fast. He felt his right-hand peg dig into the asphalt. Maybe he could power through it? Nope. He felt his rear tire losing grip. He low-sided. His bike slid out from under him and across the road into the lane for oncoming traffic. He followed just seconds behind. He was glad he was wearing leathers, gloves, and his helmet. He was also thankful that there were no cars heading his way as he careened across the road.

His riding gloves saved his hands from getting skinned up as he slid across the street. He hit the far curb with a mighty whack. An old geezer who was driving alone pulled over and checked on him.

"Are you okay, son?" he asked, helping Steve to his feet.

Truth be told, his dignity was probably more hurt than his body. It had been a very long time since he last low-sided, probably back when he still owned a sports bike.

"Ah, thanks. Motorcycle mishap," said Steve, shaking his limbs.

"Ah, you idiots ride way too fast on those contraptions. You're lucky you didn't die, son," said the old-timer.

"Hey now, it was a mechanical malfunction, buddy. I've been riding for 17 years, and I'm always safety first."

"Yes, yes, of course you are," said the old man. "You need some help with your motorbike?"

As if that guy could lift a 600 lbs machine.

"I'll be fine. Thanks for helping, mister. Much appreciated," said Steve, dusting dirt off his jeans and boots.

The old man got back in his vehicle and took off. Steve went to assess the damage to his precious bike.

Steve's Harley had a scrape down the gas tank and a ding in its rear fender. His right-hand wing mirror was destroyed, but no biggie. Surprisingly, other than that, it was working fine. He contemplated pushing it back to his house, but decided to try riding it back instead. It was just slightly too far to push back in the lunchtime sun comfortably. He was cautious, but what was the old saying? "Get thrown off the horse; the best thing you can do is get right back on it." The longer you wait, the more you freak yourself out, or so the logic went. He cruised home in first gear, ready to jump off at a moment's notice if things got squirrely, but they never did.

So it was apparent that Stefani never lifted the curse, if that was really what the problem was. Now what?

If you have a back problem, you go to a chiropractor. If you have a tooth problem, you see a dentist. So, if you have an ancient Indian curse? You had best consult with a Native American Indian, figured Steve.

He tried to think of who he had in his contacts who knew any Hopi Indians. Then he realized one of the bouncers he worked with at a nightclub was a Hopi Indian, Jacen Cloud. He would call Jacen and pick his brain.

He called Jacen and explained the situation. Jacen told him to sit tight and that he would swing by that afternoon to check things out. That was fine by Steve. He was already bruised up from the morning low-side; he had seen enough excitement for one day.

Around 4 p.m., Steve's phone went off. It was Jacen. Since when did people start texting to say they were outside as opposed to ringing the buzzer? Oh well, no biggie. Steve invited Jacen in and offered him a beer. They then sat in his living room, and he told Jacen the whole story.

Jacen listened carefully and then asked to see the bike. Steve led him to the garage, and it was probably just his imagination, but things felt "weird" in there when they entered. What hippies would call "bad vibes," it just didn't feel right.

Jacen approached Steve's bike like he was approaching a deadly snake or an alligator basking in the sun, with extreme caution.

The big man rubbed his palms together and held them outward as he slowly approached the cursed Harley.

Jacen never even touched the Harley; his hands had to be about seven to eight inches away from the bike. Jacen shuddered and stepped back quickly. He turned to leave the garage, and Steve noticed the look of fear on his face.

"Let's get out of here," he said to Steve. "There's some bad energy on your bike. Really bad."

The duo returned to Steve's living room.

"Bad?" asked Steve.

"Seriously bad," said Jacen. Even looking at him, Steve could tell the big man was shaken.

"So what do I do?" asked Steve.

"Tell me again what this guy looked like," asked Jacen.

Steve described the old medicine man.

"I can't be sure, but that sounds like Billy Crane, an old powaqa," Jacen replied.

"Wait, what? What's a powaqa?" asked Steve.

"Hmm, probably the closest terms in English would be kind of like your 'witch doctor.' Does that make sense?" asked Jacen.

"Yeah, totally does," said Steve. "How do I find this Billy Crane?"

"Hmm, I know he comes to town once a month, but from what I know, he lives on the rez," said Jacen.

"The Rez?" asked Steve.

"Oh, the reservation. The Masina Cliffs Reservation. It's out past Show Low," explained Jacen.

"Can you take me there?" asked Steve.

"Me? No, I can't," said Jacen. "You are the one who wronged him. You would have to go alone."

"Ugh, I figured you would say that," sighed Steve. "Anything else I should know?"

"Just showing up, they probably won't even let you on the reservation. Let me call my uncle and see if I can grease the wheels, so to speak," said Jacen. "You would probably need to bring him a gift, too."

"Fair enough. I figured as much," said Steve.

"And you know you are going to have to apologize," said Jacen.

"I know," said Steve. "Look, just so you know, the old man just stepped out in front of me, crossing the street. I just reacted. You must understand that."

"I get it. That's normal in Western culture. But for someone like Billy, a powerful powaqa, that would be seen as the height of disrespect," explained Jacen.

Jacen explained everything he knew about old Hopi curses and the way to find Billy Crane. He promised he would speak to his uncle that evening and then advise Steve when it would be safe for him to travel to the Masina Cliffs Reservation.

Chapter Four

True to his word, Jacen called Steve back that night. He was all set. Unlike some of the Arizona reservations that charged for guided tours, the Masina Cliffs Reservation didn't usually let just any old person wander into their lands. With the help of his uncle, Jacen had cleared the way for Steve to ride up that Saturday morning and meet with tribal powaqa Billy Crane.

Steve checked Google Maps; he would have to leave home around 6 a.m. on Saturday morning to make it to Billy's reservation by lunchtime. He adjusted his bartending schedule accordingly. Saturday rolled around, and Steve gave his bike a quick safety check and reviewed the route one more time before heading out. Despite Arizona being a Second Amendment-friendly, open-carry state, Steve decided to leave his pistol at home. Made no sense to bring it if he was on a mission of peace. He did, however, take his buck knife with him. He was confident his hosts would understand.

Traffic was fairly light when Steve rolled onto the I-17 North. Who else would be that crazy to be up and awake at 6 a.m. on a Saturday? Steve had lost count of the number of times he had gotten home at, say, 4 a.m. on Saturday morning after a Friday night of slinging drinks, then hitting an all-night diner after closeout to feed himself. Good days.

After a couple of gas station stops to fill up, take a leak, and rehydrate, Steve found himself approaching the reservation by 11 a.m. Strangely, he had no issues with his motorcycle the whole ride up. It was like it had never been cursed. Back to how it used to run. Perfectly.

Two young men were working the gates and asked him who he was there to see. First, he gave Billy Crane's name, but after seeing the look of concern on both their faces, he corrected himself and told them, "Andrew Cloud," Jacen's uncle. Satisfied with that, the guys gave him directions to find Jacen's uncle.

The residential area was about two miles away from the front gates, and Steve found Uncle Andrew's house fairly easily due to its distinct color scheme. As he was parking his bike, an older guy who looked a lot like Jacen exited the building. Steve assumed it was Jacen's uncle.

"Hello. Are you Steve?" asked the older man. Steve put out his hand for Jacen's uncle to shake. "Hi, I am Steve, Jacen's friend."

"Nice to meet you, Steve. You can call me Andrew," said Jacen's uncle.

They made small talk for a bit, then Andrew told Steve he would lead him to Billy's home. He ran back inside, got his keys, and then collected his pickup truck from the back of the property. He made sure Steve was ready to ride and took him on a quick mile drive further into the reservation to meet with Steve's nemesis, Billy Crane.

After parking up, Andrew told Steve to get off his bike but wait out front. Since Steve wanted to get this stupid curse lifted as soon as possible, he was prepared to play along, at least for now.

Andrew stepped up to the front porch, looked back to make sure Steve was off his bike and standing nearby, then knocked on the door. It took a moment, but finally, someone came to the door, opening it a crack. Steve couldn't hear what was being said, but he assumed it was about him. Then the front door shut. Andrew looked back at Steve, shrugged, then walked off the porch and back onto the street. He did a small, discreet wave and mouthed something. Steve couldn't make out what was being said but assumed it was something along the lines of "Give us a minute."

Steve and Andrew stood awkwardly on the dirt road. What was I even doing here? Questioned Steve. Was this all just a big waste of time? Maybe his bike had just malfunctioned, and he'd gotten it into his head that this old man was responsible?

Finally, the old man appeared, flanked by two younger Native American Indians. His bodyguards? His assistants? His apprentices?

As instructed, Steve waited patiently for Billy to step off his porch and onto the dirt road before he stepped forward to speak.

He apologized and explained he was upset as he had not wanted to run over Billy, who had stepped out in front of him. Billy listened but didn't say anything. He then walked over and approached Steve's motorcycle. He said a loud chant that Steve couldn't understand, and the older man held his hands up and outward to the sky. He then slowly lowered them until he had his hands on Steve's bike. Steve swore he could see some form of energy leave the bike as the old man did this. Or had he just imagined it?

Once this spectacle was over, Steve figured he could make some small talk and be on his way home. With any luck, he would be home by 6 p.m.

Billy turned and said something in a language that Steve didn't understand to his two bodyguards. One of them turned and went back inside Billy's house, reappearing moments later with what looked like two water bottles. The assistant then walked back up to Billy and handed them to the old man.

The old man then placed both bottles on the ground, crouched down, and said some words while waving his hands about over the two bottles. Finally, he got up, picked up both bottles, and handed them to his other assistant.

He spoke again to the younger men in the same language as before. It must've been some old Hopi tongue, Steve assumed.

The younger guy holding the two bottles then turned to Steve and approached him.

"Okay. Billy has attempted to remove the evil spirits that took control of your machine. He has managed to remove most of them, but one remains."

"How can one remain if he was the one who put them there?" asked Steve, sensing these guys were making this up as they went along.

"They had fed on dark energy since inhabiting your bike. They have grown stronger than expected," explained the younger man.

"Alright, so how do we get rid of them?" asked Steve.

"Here," said the younger man, handing Steve the two water bottles.

Steve took them both. One had a red cap; one had a blue cap. "Okay, what am I meant to do with these?" he asked.

Billy Crane spoke in his native tongue to the younger assistant. Steve couldn't even pick out any words. He waited for the interpretation from the younger guy.

The younger guy pointed to a mountain in the distance.

"You see that mountain?" he asked.

"Yes, of course," said Steve.

"You are to walk there. You can drink as much of the water with the blue cap as you want."

"Okay," Steve replied.

"Once you get there, scale to the top. There is only one clear path; you cannot miss it," said the assistant.

"Alright," Steve replied.

"After you get to the top, you will see a small stone structure."

"Stone structure, got it," said Steve.

"You will sit in that structure and then consume all the liquid in the bottle with the red cap," explained Billy's assistant.

"Then what happens?" asked Steve.

"You will spend the night there. In the morning, your problem will be solved."

It sounded like nonsense to Steve, but these guys seemed genuine. He had come this far; he might as well follow through.

"Alright, so walk to the mountain, climb it, find your stone structure, sit in it, drink the liquid in the bottle with the red cap, spend the night, and come back in the morning. Correct?"

"Correct," smiled the man, looking over to Billy Crane to make sure it was indeed correct. Billy looked back and nodded.

"Well, if that's all there is to it, I guess I'll get going," said Steve to his new friends.

"Very well then. May your gods go with you," said Billy's assistant.

Steve took one last look back. Jacen's uncle gave Steve a nod of approval, and the men watched as he headed toward the mountain on the horizon.

It was early afternoon, and the sun hit hard, much harder than standing in the shade of Billy Crane's front porch.

Steve took small swigs from the blue-capped bottle as he walked along. As he got closer to the mountain, it appeared bigger and bigger, much bigger than he had initially anticipated. "Fuck this," thought Steve. "Why me? This is some bullshit," he trudged on.

He was starting to sweat; he kept drinking from the bottle. It was only when he took a long swig from the bottle that he realized somewhere along the way, he was also drinking from the red-capped bottle as well.

Shit, did that mess up the Hopi medicine man's plans or what?

Steve wasn't sure. He kept walking.

After a good two hours, he finally made it to the base of the mountain. It didn't take him long to find the small path the guys had spoken about. He started his climb to the top. As he started to climb, he swore he saw some purple flashes in the sky. WTF?

Then it dawned on him. The red-capped bottle had to be some form of psychedelic. He had taken LSD a bunch back in high school, and he knew it wasn't that. Magic mushrooms, maybe? What did the Native Indians take? Peyote? Was it peyote? He wasn't sure. Regardless of what it was, he was starting to trip. "Oh great," thought Steve, "I'm starting to climb a mountain, and I'm beginning to trip balls." I can just see the headlines now, "Biker found dead after falling off ancient Indian sacred site."

He was now halfway up the climb. He risked a look back. He could barely make out Billy Crane's property in the distance. He was way, way out there now. If someone told him he was alone on some far-flung planet in outer space right now, he would have probably believed them. There was nothing around. He continued his climb, only stopping to drink from the blue-capped water bottle.

Finally, he made it to the top. He was wiped out. Even though he had a path to the top, it was still physically exhausting. Now he had to locate this structure, which they told him would be up there. To the left or to the right?

The path to the right didn't seem to go far, so he decided to investigate to the left first.

The path was small and seemed to zigzag all over the place. Who made this path? Mountain goats? He continued on until he found a stone structure. It was a low stone wall, maybe four feet tall, built in a circle with an opening like a "doorway." Steve imagined that at some point, there was probably mud or some crude form of cement to hold all of the stonework in place that had dried up and disappeared over a period of time. How long had this been here? He guessed a good four or five hundred years. Well, this was clearly the spot.

He entered, pulled off his boots and socks to give his feet a chance to breathe, and sat down.

Now what? he assumed. Just finish the rest of the liquid in the red-capped bottle and see what happens.

Chapter Five

Steve sat down in the ancient structure. The psychedelic trip was really starting to hit hard now. All around him, primitive bugs and critters crawled, but when he tried to grab them, all he caught was a handful of sand. Somewhere near the top of the mountain, an owl was hooting. With every "hoot," the sky changed color: blue, purple, orange, green. Steve was flying high but still coherent enough to know he was under the influence.

How was this going to help lift the curse on his bike? If anything, it might scramble his brains more, but Steve could see no way this would help him. A huge waste of time.

His trip was becoming more intense now. The sky was swirling in colors. In fact, Steve had to lie in the dirt, face toward the sky, as he could no longer continue to hold his body upright. He stared in awe at the early evening sky with his mouth wide open, unable to close it. He was flying high.

Steve wasn't sure if he had blacked out or passed out. He had lost all track of time; the powerful hallucinogen had disabled his entire body. He was just a brain now. His arms and legs didn't move. Couldn't be moved. Even his jaw hung slack on his face. He was in awe of the night sky, heck, of the universe now. If anyone had come across him in this ancient stone fort, they would have thought of him as retarded, possibly worse. There was no way he could interact with another person. Possibly forever?

Steve hadn't taken LSD since high school, and this was certainly no LSD trip. Something much more ancient, more powerful, and wilder. But he did recall advice he had given friends, and people had given him, back when he used to consume LSD at parties and stuff: just go with it. The more you resist the effects of the drug, the worse your trip's gonna be. He lay on his back and took it all in. He was definitely still peaking. He had no idea how much time had passed.

Finally, the drug seemed to change its grip on Steve's body. He got back use of his arms and legs and even his face. He reached over, wiped the drool from his mouth, and tried to sit up. Was it over? Nope. He was still seeing a kaleidoscope of color in the night sky. At least he could sit up now and somewhat function as a human being.

He thought about getting up, maybe drinking some water in the blue-capped bottle, but that still felt like a million miles away, even though it was just outside the stone circle.

Was this it? Was it over? he asked himself as he sat in the dirt.

Just as Steve thought that, two small hooded men walked into the stone circle, for lack of a better description, the first thing that came to Steve's mind was "leprechauns" or elves, even.

He smiled. "Why hello there."

"Hello, Steve. We have been expecting you," said the two leprechaun-type guys in unison.

"You're funny," laughed Steve. For some reason, he couldn't stop smiling at the newcomers.

"Thank you, Steve. Do you know why you have summoned us here tonight?" asked one of the two little men.

"I summoned you?" asked Steve, somewhat confused. Wait. Were they part of this acid trip?

"Yes. You called, and we came," answered the other diminutive elf.

"Oh, I did? Oops. Sorry. My bad," said Steve, still grinning like an idiot.

"Well? Do you want our help or not?" asked the first elf, starting to get annoyed by Steve's foolishness.

"Well, yeah! If you don't mind," said Steve, worried his tiny friends might leave.

"What do you need, friend?" asked the second elf.

"My bike is cursed," said Steve, feeling stupid saying it out loud. "Can you help me?"

The two elves talked to each other for a moment, then turned back to Steve.

"I think we can help you," said the first elf.

"Okay, great. Just tell me what I have to do," said Steve.

"I have the solution for you, but you probably are not going to like it," said the first elf.

"Okay, try me. I am ready to do anything to rid my motorcycle of that evil spirit or whatever it is," said Steve to the two leprechauns or whatever they were.

"You have to give up your bike and your outlaw ways. That's the only way to lift your curse, my friend," said the second elf. "Only then will things change for you."

"What? Are you kidding me?" asked Steve. "That makes no sense."

"It does if you think about it," said the first elf.

"How do you figure?" asked Steve, starting to get really pissed off.

"Well, think of it this way: the love you take is equal to the love you make," said the second elf.

"That sounds like some half-assed Beatles lyric or something," said Steve, really starting to get pissed off.

"The choice is yours, friend," both elves said at the same time while standing there with real creepy smiles on their faces.

"Yeah, well. I have a lot to think about then, don't I?" said Steve, barely hiding his annoyance.

"That you do, friend," said the first elf. "You should sleep on it."

"I think I will," said Steve.

"We will go then," said the two elves. "Goodbye, friend. I am sure we will see you again one day."

And just like that, the two elves disappeared.

Steve was annoyed now. He liked those little guys, but he felt they were talking crap. Whatever the psychedelic he had consumed was, it was starting to wear off. All of a sudden, Steve found himself incredibly exhausted.

Steve lay down and got himself into a comfy position. Within moments, he was out.

When he woke up, the sun was rising in the east. He had survived the night without being attacked by coyotes, mountain lions, snakes, or scorpions. He could tell the drug was still in his bloodstream, but just a very small dose. He felt good enough to attempt to climb back down the mountain.

He checked the two water bottles. The red-capped one was empty, but he still had half the blue-capped water bottle left. He was so thirsty. He took a decent swig and collected his socks and boots, shaking his boots first just in case a scorpion had crept into one of them. Thankfully, nothing was there.

Steve grabbed both bottles and started his way back down the makeshift mountain pass. The last thing he needed now, after surviving a night in the wilderness, was to slip and fall on his way back home.

He knew he was high as a kite the night before, but his encounter with the two little leprechauns played on his mind. Were they real? They had to be a hallucination, right? He was talking to them, and they were talking back. Maybe they were real. He should have looked for little footprints in the dirt, but it was too late now.

As he made the long walk back to Billy Crane's place, he thought about his options. Why should he change? He had always been a good and honourable man. Done right by the ones who loved him and were ready to stand by those beliefs. He loved his motorcycle. To give that all up would be a betrayal of his true self. That said, he couldn't risk what happened to him earlier in the week happening again and again. He had a decision to make.

Someone at Billy's house must have been watching out for him. As soon as he got closer to the property, the three men came out of the house and walked to greet him.

"Good morning," said Billy. "You survived."

"Morning, Mr. Crane," said Steve. "I brought your two bottles back to you."

Steve took another long swig from the blue-capped bottle before handing both over to one of Billy's assistants.

"So how did it go?" asked Billy.

"Eh, alright, I guess," Steve replied.

"Well, what did they tell you?" asked Billy, with a knowing smile on his face.

"They told me how to lift the curse," Steve replied, making a beeline for his bike.

"Ah, okay," said Billy. "I had a feeling they would."

Steve checked his Harley over. From what he could tell, no one had touched it or tampered with it. He started it up and let it idle for a minute.

"There's just one problem," said Steve.

"What's that?" asked Billy Crane.

"I can't change, and I won't change. I'm just going to take my chances with her," he said, nodding toward his bike.

"What? You are?" asked Billy incredulously.

"Yeah. Why not? All of life is a risk. If I give up my lifestyle, if I give up my motorcycle, I might as well be dead anyway. So I'm just gonna live my life," Steve replied.

Billy seemed aghast. His two assistants seemed amused.

"Yeah. So listen, man. No hard feelings, eh? Thanks for all your help, and for the drugs, whatever they were. It's been real, but I gotta go," said Steve.

"Very well, my friend. Be safe, and may your god go with you," said Billy.

"Thanks. And Billy," said Steve.

"What?" asked Billy.

"If you're ever back down in Phoenix, look me up, and we'll have a beer together."

"Thanks, my friend. Be safe," said Billy.

Steve got on his Harley, squeezed in the clutch, kicked it in gear, gave the guys a final wave goodbye, and took off, heading back toward the Valley of the Sun.

Cactus Crown

Elliot Vance had everything a Brooklyn hipster could want: apartment lofts with exposed brick, vintage leather jackets that cost more than rent, and a trust fund that made bartending "for the aesthetic" possible. But after his third cocaine arrest in a year, the Vance family trust decided enough was enough. His uncle bought him a one-way airline ticket to Arizona.

"Out there, you'll find yourself," his mother said, sliding the boarding pass across the reclaimed wood kitchen table.

Elliot rolled his eyes. "Find myself in what, a cactus?"

A week later, he was standing in a blistering Tucson bus depot near the airport with one duffel bag, wearing his favorite $400 boots.

That's when the trouble really started.

He didn't know it, but Elliot bore a striking resemblance to Jack "Crow" Medina, the recently surfaced twenty-something president of the Red Vultures Motorcycle Club. Crow was infamous: a ghost who'd risen fast through blood, fire, and desert law. Rumor was he'd just gotten out of a Yuma lockup and was rallying his men for a new chapter in southern Arizona.

When Elliot walked into a roadside bar to escape the heat, every biker in the place went quiet. Men with knives tattooed on their throats set their beers down. A waitress whispered, "Crow."

Elliot tried to laugh it off. "Uh, no, I'm Elliot. From, "

A hand clapped his shoulder, heavy as iron. "We thought you were dead, brother," the biker said, eyes glinting. "Welcome home."

By nightfall, Elliot was riding bitch on a chopper, dust in his teeth, trying to remember not to scream as the desert blurred by.

For three days, he lived like an outlaw. He sat at firelit tables while men whispered about shipments and scores. He drank tequila straight from the bottle while women draped themselves across his lap, thinking they were lying with a king. Every time someone asked him for orders, Elliot leaned on the only skill New York had ever given him: bullshit.

"Patience, boys," he said, nodding sagely. "Timing's everything."

It almost worked. Until Crow himself came back.

The real Crow walked into camp one night, lean, scarred, and very much alive. The bikers froze, torn between the leader they thought they had and the impostor who'd bluffed his way into their loyalty.

Elliot felt the desert close in around him. For once in his life, irony wasn't funny.

Crow's eyes locked on him. "You've been wearing my face, city boy."

Elliot swallowed. "Look, I, uh, misunderstood?"

The club waited for blood. Instead, Crow laughed, a low, dangerous sound. "You got guts, I'll give you that. But guts don't keep you alive out here."

By dawn, Elliot was dumped at the edge of the highway, duffel bag at his feet, Harley tire tracks fading into the horizon. His boots were ruined, his throat was raw, and his whole body shook from three days of desert fire.

But for the first time in his life, Elliot Vance didn't feel like a fraud.

His family had sent him to Arizona to straighten out. Instead, Arizona had nearly buried him alive.

And maybe, just maybe, that was the first real thing he'd ever done.

Ghost Riders

Chapter One

Jack "Rattlesnake" Mercer was enjoying a beer at his favorite biker bar, the infamous Filthy Hogg Saloon on Cave Creek Road in Sunnyslope, Phoenix. It had been a long-ass day at work, and an ice-cold beer was his reward. A few regulars recognized him chilling on the back patio and came up to say hello. Life was good. No matter how tough a day at work got, a cold beer would always put things right. Why people would go on antidepressants when beer was available was lost on him.

Halfway through his first beer, his club brother "Slim" Dalton hit the patio seeking out Jack. Slim had been a fully patched member of Jack's motorcycle club, the Desert Saints MC, for a little over a year now. Before that, he was a prospect for six months and maybe a hangaround for a year. Young dude, full of energy and a solid cat. In his hands was a tray with two beers and two shots. He sat down and fist-bumped Jack.

"Good to see ya, brother," said Slim.

"Likewise," Jack replied, holding his shot glass in the air to salute Slim. Slim held up his whiskey shot, too, returning the gesture. "Cheers, bro."

Jack's whiskey tasted better than his beer, and all the stress of his day was forgotten.

"So, you're coming, right?" asked Slim.

"Yeah, sure," Jack replied, then realized he had no clue what Slim was talking about. "Wait, what are we talking about?"

"Ross's funeral!" Slim exclaimed.

"Oh, yeah, of course. Don't worry, I hadn't forgotten," Jack replied. "I just wasn't sure what you were talking about."

"Yeah, that's cool," said Slim. "This Sunday."

"I know, bro. I know," said Jack.

"You know what's weird?" asked Slim.

"What?" said Jack.

"I read this morning that another biker got knocked down by one of those self-driving cars on the 101 last night. He didn't die, but he's banged up pretty bad. In the hospital right now," said Slim.

"Those fucking cars. I don't trust 'em, bro," said Jack. "Honestly, the first time I saw one, I thought it was one of those Google Street Map cars, you know, the ones with all the cameras all over them?"

"Yeah, I get ya," Slim replied.

"Then, when I pulled up next to it, there was no one driving," said Jack. "I nearly fell off my scoot."

"Ha ha, yeah, I bet," laughed Slim. "They're like those Johnny Cabs from that Arnold movie Total Recall."

"I remember that movie," Jack replied. "Hey, I tell ya right now, I trust those Johnny Cabs more than those Aegens. Straight up."

The Aegens were self-driving cars, much like an Uber, but driven entirely by AI, with no human on board. Aegis Mobility, a corporation leading the self-driving car boom, was using Phoenix as its test market. If all went well here, they could start expanding into other metropolises like LA and Dallas.

Publicly, the Aegis corporation boasted about its safety record, but inside the tech firm, things were very, very different.

Chapter Two

Leah Ramirez loved data. No, she really loved data. Leah grew up in Phoenix, Arizona, and moved to Northern California's Silicon Valley on a partial scholarship to prestigious Stanford University, studying computer science before getting a fully paid internship with the Aegis Corporation. Led by eccentric entrepreneur Mr Bishop, the company had grown in leaps and bounds in recent years with its mind-blowing advancements in both quantum computing and artificial intelligence. Determined to make more of an impact than both Bill Gates and Elon Musk on the world, Mr Bishop's Aegis was on a mission to be number one.

Most people thought Stanford University was in Palo Alto, but it was actually, surprise -surprise, the town of Stanford. Who knew? After spending four years bouncing around between labs in the tech trifecta of Mountain View, Cupertino, and Palo Alto, Leah was one of the first to jump at the chance to relocate to Mesa, Arizona, when Mr Bishop announced he would be breaking ground on a new tech headquarters back in Arizona. It wasn't just Aegis setting up shop in Mesa; Apple, Google, and Meta (Facebook and Instagram) all had offices there, too.

While she was paid well as an intern at Aegis, the cost of living in Silicon Valley was crippling. The other deciding factor on returning to Arizona was, well, nightlife. Locally, everything shut down at 6 pm in Palo Alto. If you forgot to get your groceries, you were pretty much out of luck, as there was nothing open. You might as well be living in some small town in the Midwest. Sure, San Francisco was about an hour's drive north of the valley, but with the long hours everyone put in at the office, driving an hour to see a live band play, and then driving another hour home at the end of the night was just too exhausting. So back to Arizona she went, this time as a fully paid-up member of staff.

Mr Bishop had seen what Uber had done to the taxi cab industry, and he was determined to be as much of a disruptor to Uber and Lyft as they were to Yellow cabs. Self-driving cars were the future, he had decided, and he was wagering everything on being first to market.

Leah's team was tasked with risk assessment, and she was tasked with traffic analysis and investigation reports on Mr Bishop's self-driving cars. The days were long, often coming to the office at 7 am and not leaving till 10 at night. She recalled a colleague in their Northern California campus who hadn't bothered to rent an expensive apartment; he had simply used all of the campus's resources: in-house restaurants, gyms, shower facilities, and slept in his car at night. He saved thousands and thousands of dollars over the course of three years, enough to quit, buy a house for cash in the Midwest, and drop out of the rat race. He was one of the smart ones.

Leah was reviewing the latest data reports for the Phoenix Metro area. Another accident? That can't be right. She generated an additional report using different search parameters and, yep, it came up again. How could this be? This wasn't in any of their public reports; something was wrong here. She had to bring this to her manager, George. He needed to know.

Logging into the company's workflow system, she saw that George had an availability for "2 pm" the following afternoon. She took that opportunity to book a thirty-minute meeting with him.

At 1:55 pm the following afternoon, Leah grabbed a latte from the company coffee spot and headed to George's office, which was upstairs and on the other side of the building from where her team was based. It probably made more sense in Leah's mind if he was at least based in an office near their team, but hey, what did she know about corporate politics?

She waited until her Apple Watch told her it was one minute to two and knocked on George's door. Her boss hated tardiness, and she figured being slightly early made more sense than being even a minute late. She waited until she heard him say, "Come in," and entered. Without looking up, he told her to have a seat, and so she did.

Finally, he put down the report he was studying.

"Hi, Leah," he said.

"George," she replied.

"You called this meeting, so how can I help you?" he asked.

"Oh yes," said Leah. "I was reviewing performance reports last night, and I found a list of accidents that were not officially listed on our mainframe."

"What?" asked George. Leah couldn't figure out if he was annoyed or surprised.

"Yes. If you run a regular accident report, it shows only 3 accidents for every 1000 rides, but if you refine the search parameters, it shows more than 50 accidents per 1000 rides," said Leah proudly.

"Let me see that," said George. He reached over and grabbed the printed report that Leah had brought with her to the meeting.

He studied the reams and reams of data for a good two minutes before looking back at Leah.

"Ah, yes, this seems like some sort of glitch in the program. That's all," said George. "I'll have Davis from our programming team run some fail-safes and get this sorted out. Thanks for bringing it to our attention, Ms Ramirez."

"But..." started Leah.

"No buts, Leah. Consider the issue resolved," George gestured to the door. "Thanks for your time today. Please leave it with me and get back to that charging station analysis you promised me. Thanks."

Leah grabbed her report and left.

What a jerk, she thought. Dismissing me like that. Probably because I'm a woman, I'll show him.

After 5 pm, some of her co-workers started to finish off for the day and said their goodbyes. By 6 pm, most of her department had left for the day. Leah had a thought. Aegis had proprietary software that could access police and hospital mainframes without permission. Was it legal? Duh, of course not, but tech companies like Aegis operated within a gray area at times, doing what they pleased. Always better to ask for forgiveness than ask for permission was standard operating procedure for Mr Bishop and his cronies.

Leah gained access to the Phoenix Metro's police computer system with a couple of shift keystrokes. Sadly, it was that easy. She could access files and reports but not edit them. She started searching for self-driving vehicle accidents. Then, messing with the search terms, she tried Uber, Tesla, Waymo, and Aegis.

She logged out and then quickly accessed the city's main hospital records. Once again, she worked on the search terms until she was satisfied with all the data she had pulled up. She downloaded all her findings. Then she logged out of their search software. It was late, and she was tired. She decided to make a quick backup of her findings onto a small flash drive and figured she could fully analyze her findings tomorrow on her lunch break.

It was now after 9 pm, and she was mentally and physically exhausted. It had been a long day. Time to get home, get some sleep, and do it all again tomorrow.

She arrived at work just before 9 am. After grabbing some coffee, she sat down at her desk and made a quick review of all the tasks she and her team would have to tackle today.

Leah was deep in thought when she looked up to see that asshole George standing there with two of Aegis's security personnel.

"Ms Ramirez, can you come with us, please?" said one of the two security guards.

"Uh...what's this about?" she asked.

"Just come with us. Thank you," said the guard.

Leah got up, shrugged at some of her coworkers, and followed the trio to a corner office.

"Sit down, please, Leah," said George after the door was closed.

"What's going on?" she asked.

"Did you not recall me asking you to leave the accident reports yesterday, Leah?" asked George.

"Uh, yes?" she replied.

"My computer pinged last night, telling me you were still pulling data on this," George replied.

"It was after office hours," said Leah.

"Doesn't matter. I told you to leave it. I can't have this type of insubordination on my floor," said George, starting to get angry.

"But, I" said Leah.

"Look, let me stop you right there. You're not fired..."

"What? You're firing me?" gasped Leah.

"No, I said you're not fired," said George. "But obviously, you have been under a lot of pressure lately. I am putting you on two weeks' paid leave. Starting right now."

"But," said Leah.

"No buts. These two gentlemen will escort you back to your workspace. Please collect any personal belongings and leave the building. I shall see you in two weeks. Ideally well rested. Good day." George got up and left the private office.

Leah walked back in stunned silence with her two escorts, grabbed her handbag and cup of coffee, and left for the day.

What the actual fuck? she thought as she drove home. What the fuck?

Chapter Three

Jack arrived at Ross's funeral just before 2 p.m. He looked for Slim but didn't see him immediately among the mourners. He did spot two of his club brothers from the Desert Saints Motorcycle Club, Shorty and Tex. Jack approached them and gave them both a big bear hug. This was surreal. Jack had attended his share of funerals over the years, but it was usually someone killed doing some stupid thing, like riding home completely wasted. Never buy a fully computerized car. Was this how the Terminators and Skynet started the robot war? Thought Jack, semi-seriously.

Finally, he spotted Slim. He was with his grieving mother and what looked like Slim's grandparents. He waited until Slim had pulled himself away from his family members and waved. Slim spotted him and headed over.

"Hey, man. Thanks so much for coming," said Slim, hugging Jack. "You see Shorty and Tex are here?"

"Yeah. Spoke to them," Jack replied. "How are you holding up?"

"I'm dealing with it, man. Truth be told, it's harder dealing with my mom and her folks," said Slim.

Jack looked back over at Slim's grieving family members. "Oh, I bet," he said in a show of emotional support.

"Hey, you know what's weird?" asked Slim.

"What, man?" Jack replied.

"Another biker was killed by one of those damn Johnny Cabs last night."

"What? That wasn't on the news," Jack was stunned.

"Andy was working emergency towing last night. Got called to the scene of an accident. One of those Aegis mobiles struck a biker. Basically ran him over. Straight-up murder, bro."

"Get out of here," Jack replied.

"Yeah. Some corporate dude turned up from Aegis to offer Andy $1,000 to keep his mouth shut. Told the dude to go fuck himself," said Slim.

"Well, damn," Jack replied. "Something isn't right here."

"I know! I know!" said Slim. "I've been trying to tell you."

"We gotta do something," said Jack. "If this were a rival club killing our boys, we would shut 'em down right away. I just don't know how we should proceed."

"I read somewhere they are doing a town hall meetup with the public tomorrow night in downtown Phoenix. I was planning on attending," said Slim.

"No shit. Well, you know I'll be there, bro. I got you covered," said Jack.

"Thanks, brother," Slim replied. "I appreciate that."

Chapter Four

Leah was furious. She had never been given two weeks of paid leave before. How did this happen? What was up with George's butt to treat her like that? Sheesh.

She spent the morning fuming, then finally it dawned on her. Hold up, she was getting paid to stay home? She should see this as a vacation, not a punishment.

Once she had a clearer head, she also realized that she still had the flash drive she had taken home last night. She grabbed her laptop, plugged in the tiny drive, and opened up the file folder.

She was officially off duty. She could investigate anything she wanted in her spare time, on her own computer. Right?

Digging deeper into the files and cross-checking with previous work files she had stored at home, Leah discovered something big. The vehicle's AI algorithms prioritized "road safety" (as they should), but deep in the coding, she found that motorcyclists were deemed "chaotic variables" and expendable. Expendable? Was she reading that right? Surely they didn't mean "expendable" expendable? Whoever wrote this must have meant something else. This could not be right. Worse, Aegis Mobility had secretly programmed some of the fleet to eliminate "unnecessary risks" to maximize passenger safety statistics, including human riders.

She nearly jumped off her cozy couch when she read that. It had to be a joke. Who would have approved this? It made zero sense. All safety protocols had to be approved by four separate departments, and ultimately would have required Mr. Bishop's sign-off. This could not be true. She ran the same analysis programs twice more and still came back with the same results. This was crazy. She needed to tell someone. But who?

Chapter Five

Aegis held its "Town Hall" meeting at the courthouse situated in Downtown Phoenix. Jack met Slim at Jack's Mesa home before riding their Harleys over to the city center. They easily found street parking and walked the final block to the courthouse.

There were probably 250 or so people in attendance, with a handful of reporters and journalists filling the first two rows of the conference room.

Jack noted upon arrival that microphones were set up near the stage in front of both the left and right rows, separating the seating. That had to be for the open mic question-and-answer section of the afternoon. He figured they would be wise to grab seats nearby so they would have the first chance to ask questions of the Aegis representatives.

A couple of different "Executive Vice Presidents" came out and gave their cute little presentations on how Aegis was revolutionizing travel, some stuff on car ownership, and then safety for their female passengers. It all felt very self-congratulatory in Jack's mind and a load of grandstanding. Finally, it was time for the general public to step up and ask questions of the various executives. Jack nudged Slim and gestured toward the nearest microphone. By the time Slim got out of his seat and made his way over, he was at least third in line on the left side of the building to ask questions.

The moderator started on the left side, then switched to the first person in line on the right side of the building, and then back to the left side again. By the time they got to Slim, about fifteen minutes must have passed according to Jack's reckoning.

Finally, Slim stepped up to the mic.

"You, sir, do you have a question?" asked the moderator.

Slim coughed and cleared his throat.

"Yes, I have a question. What does Aegis have to say about the high amount of motorcycle-related accidents their cars seem to be involved in?"

"Ah, good question. Let's hear from our head of safety, Mr. Gavin Martin. Take it away, Gavin."

Aegis's Mr. Martin leaned into his microphone.

"Well, first of all, thank you for the question. Secondly, I have to disagree with you. I would go as far as saying Aegis has a fantastic safety record. In fact, our customers' safety is our number one priority in our books. Just because a couple of thrill-seeking motorcyclists collide near our driverless cars doesn't mean it's the fault of our cutting-edge technology. That's unfair."

Jack could tell by the look on Slim's face that he was quite taken aback by the reply.

"I'm sorry, I have to disagree with you," said Slim. "I would say 48 motorcycle-related accidents in the last twelve months is more than a 'couple.' Wouldn't you agree?"

"Ah, what? 48 incidents? I am not sure where you got that number from," asked Mr. Martin incredulously.

"I've spoken to many friends and family members of riders killed or injured in Phoenix," Slim replied.

"Ah, so second-hand testimony and a friend of a friend telling you tales," huffed Mr. Martin. "Wouldn't you say that's hardly the basis of solid, scientific data? Is it?"

"Uh, what?" stammered Slim. "No, I have this on good authority from various families!" A few people sniggered quietly in the audience. It was clear to Jack that Aegis's Mr. Martin had heard the mocking laughter and was quite convinced he was winning the crowd over, dismissing Slim's claims.

"I am very sorry, sir, but 'good authority' is only one step away from whispers and rumors. Unless you have any further statistics, I would ask you to step down so someone else can talk."

Slim looked defeated, deflated, and confused. Jack realized the stress of losing his brother still weighed heavily on the poor guy.

Suddenly, a woman's voice spoke up from the right-hand side of the room. The entire room, en masse, turned and looked over.

"Actually, I have all the data here," a woman announced, waving a stack of papers in her right hand. "That man is absolutely correct."

Some of the attendees gasped amongst themselves.

"Who the hell are you?" snapped Aegis's Mr. Martin.

"Never mind that. I have all the police and hospital reports here. This man is quite correct. Aegis vehicles have been striking, injuring, and killing motorcycle riders at an alarming rate," said the dark-haired young woman.

"She works at Aegis," Jack heard someone murmur in the crowd.

"Let me see that," said Slim from the other side of the room.

"Yes, I need to see that too," said Mr. Martin from the stage.

Slim pushed his way down a row of seated attendees to approach the woman on the right side of the room.

At the same time, the Aegis lackey on stage gave a nod, and two security workers who had been standing on either side of the stage started heading in the same direction as the woman.

Jack had been in enough bar fights to be able to read a room correctly. Things were about to go south very, very fast. He grabbed his riding gear and started making his way toward the woman as well.

Chapter Six

Slim made it over to the woman speaking before Jack did.

"Let me see that," he demanded, reaching for her papers. Shocked and acting on instincts, she pulled her hand behind her back to keep everything out of his reach.

Meanwhile, the two Aegis security goons were pushing their way through the crowd to get at both the woman and Slim. By now, most of the people in the room were getting to their feet, either to make a hasty exit or to get a better look at the chaos unfolding in front of them. Jack couldn't tell which.

The woman, trying to keep her papers out of Slim's reach, turned and made her way to the exit doors on the right side of the building. Slim, being Slim, well, he gave chase. Jack started moving after Slim. The two beefy security guards were chasing all of them.

The woman pushed the exit door to escape. It must have been one of those fire-exit doors, as all of a sudden the alarms started going off. The entire room panicked and started making their way for the exits, too. People were running about like chickens with their heads cut off. Slim followed the woman out the door. Jack gave chase.

Jack exited the building to be greeted by the sight of Slim talking to the woman. Behind them, a surge of people, including the two security guards, filed out of the building as the alarms blared in the background. Traffic outside ground to a halt as people stopped and stared, trying to figure out what was happening.

"Quick, this way," shouted Jack, leading both the unnamed woman and Slim toward where they had parked their Harleys a block away. The side of the building and the front were now flooded with people. Jack was relieved that they had parked a block away, giving them a chance to get away without any issues.

"Hey, we're being followed," said Slim, looking back. The two security guards were pushing their way through the crowds of people to get to them.

"What's your name?" asked Jack of the woman.

"Leah," she said as they strode quickly toward the bikers' parked machines.

"Jack," he replied. "And that's Slim."

They reached their scoots. Jack swung his right leg over and fired up his Harley.

"Quick, Leah, jump on," he said.

The woman looked horrified. Jack wasn't sure if it was the idea of jumping on the back of a motorcycle or racing away with two strange men she had just met. But the moment she saw the security guards closing in, she dropped any sort of reservations she had and clambered onto the back of Jack's bike. Confident she was properly on, he kicked his bike in gear and let out the clutch. They peeled away from the curb just as the first of the security guards arrived. A moment later, and he would have grabbed them.

Jack knew that Slim knew the drill. In emergency situations, when there was no time to communicate a plan, the Desert Saints Motorcycle Club would split up and reconvene at a coffee shop in Scottsdale. A coffee shop and not a biker bar? Simple. If law enforcement were after them, where would be the first place they would check? Notorious biker bars like the Filthy Hogg Saloon, of course. Why make it easy for them? They looped around the block, avoiding the congested street in front of the courthouse, and started riding North.

Jack saw Slim trying to get his attention. What was he pointing at?

Jack turned his head to see two large Explorer SUVs heading toward them at a high rate of speed. These were not regular road ragers; these had to be Aegis security people. They were clearly in hot pursuit.

As they raced North, Jack went through all the options in his head. His Harley was not a sports bike. He was never going to outrun two high-powered SUVs, especially not with a passenger. What advantage did a bike have over a car? He couldn't outrun them; he had to outmaneuver them. Where could he go, though?

He tried to think about what he was familiar with in this neighborhood. He knew there were some car dealerships ahead in a few blocks. Maybe there?

He gave Slim a hand signal indicating they should split up: Slim to go right, and he would go left. Slim nodded, well-versed in the Desert Saints' escape-and-evasion tactics. At the next set of traffic lights, Slim took a right and Jack continued to race North. He looked back. Dammit, they didn't take the bait. They were definitely after this woman, Leah. He was in trouble. He had to come up with a plan, and fast.

Chapter Seven

Jack found himself on 16th Street heading North. Thankfully, there was enough traffic to delay the goons chasing them. One advantage a bike had in a car chase was that it could maneuver through congested traffic. These Aegis security goons didn't have the jurisdiction that cops had to turn on their cherries and berries and their sirens to clear the roads. These guys had to push and shove their way past cars to get to him. That said, they were closing in. It was only a matter of a minute or two before they ran Jack and Leah off the road.

While the plus side to a car-versus-bike chase was the bike's maneuverability, the downside was that if it came to a war of gross tonnage, an SUV was going to beat his Harley every time. He had to come up with something fast.

Then he remembered: the canals were near here. He could find a way to access the canals, but their SUVs couldn't follow them. Phoenix was both the oldest and one of the youngest cities in the United States. Over two thousand years ago, the Hohokam Indians occupied the land that is now called Phoenix and built an intricate canal system across the entire Valley of the Sun to irrigate their crops. Over 135 miles of canals crisscross the Phoenix metro area. No one knows exactly when and why they left, but they had at least been in the valley since the time before Christ. The European settlers, seeing the remnants of the canals, thought this would be a great place to build the new city. The city rose from the flames of the old, much like the mythical Phoenix, hence the name.

Jack slowed as he found an entrance to the canals. It was big enough for bicyclists or joggers, butnot   large SUVs.

"Hang on!" he shouted at Leah as he maneuvered his Harley between the gates to the canals.

She gripped his waist tighter.

As they passed the gates, he could hear brakes squealing behind them. They had just made it in time. He kicked his bike up a gear and raced up the designated jogging/bike path. A yuppie walking his dog along the side of the canal jumped out of the way, dragging his dog with him. Jack felt bad, but he had no choice but to continue on.

In this part of Phoenix, the streets were laid out in a grid-like fashion, much like Manhattan, New York. The canal system, however, ran diagonally across the grid, making it nearly impossible to follow without a helicopter or a drone.

He figured he would run the canals a couple of miles and look for an exit near a freeway where he could circle back along the 101 toward Scottsdale.

Finally, Jack found a way to exit the canal system and get onto the I-17 North. No sign of the Aegis goons. Like he figured, it would have been next to impossible to follow them without air support. Within 20 minutes, he was working his way into Scottsdale and their rendezvous point with Slim.

As he slowed down to enter the coffee shop car park, Jack breathed a sigh of relief when he spotted Slim's bike parked away in the corner. Out of sight from the street, clever boy. He glided across the car park and parked next to Slim's Harley. He shut down his bike, then tapped Leah on the leg to signal for her to dismount. Once he was confident she was off, he did the same.

"You okay?" he asked.

"Yeah," she replied. "Thanks for the ride. God knows what those thugs would have done to me if they had caught me."

"No problem," said Jack. "Let's go grab some coffee, and why don't you tell us why they want those papers so badly?"

Chapter Eight

Jack and Leah entered the coffee shop. Jack didn't even bother looking for Slim; he knew damn well the man would be holed up in a back booth with his eyes watching the door. He went straight to the counter and asked Leah what she wanted to drink.

He then ordered himself the largest cappuccino they had on offer. He usually tried to stop drinking coffee in the afternoons as it kept him awake at night, but this time, he felt he needed it.

After he ordered, he looked, and sure enough, there was Slim sitting in the back corner. He pointed him out to Leah and told her to go sit with Slim while he waited for their orders to be served. He would bring both coffees over once they were ready.

When Jack arrived at their booth, Slim and Leah were making small talk. He sat down and slid Leah her latte. She thanked him, then pulled the cap off so she could blow on it.

He decided to leave the lid on and wait for it to cool down on its own.

Turning to Leah, he asked, "So what's got those tech goons so hot and bothered?"

"What? Oh! Aegis security," said Leah.

"Yeah. The ones who wanted to run us down, remember?"

"I have proof," said Leah.

"Proof of what?" asked Slim.

"These cars. You know, the self-driving ones, right?" said Leah.

"Yeah, they killed my brother," said Slim.

"I have proof that they were programmed not to avoid motorcyclists."

"What?" asked Jack.

"Yes. I used to work for Aegis. I found this information buried deep in the car's programming code."

"I knew it!" exclaimed Slim. "See! I told you these guys are killers."

"Well, I don't know if I would go that far," said Leah.

"You JUST told us that they are programmed to kill riders," fumed Slim.

"No! I said they were programmed not to avoid hitting motorcycle riders," corrected Leah.

"Okay," said Jack.

"Well, THAT I can prove. Maybe they are programmed to kill you guys?" said Leah, shrugging her shoulders.

"Let me see that," said Jack, grabbing the file folder from Leah.

He flicked through page after page of data, trying to find something that would make sense to a layman like himself.

Then he found it. In the "road safety" section. There it was plain as day: "Chaotic variables," "Expendable," "Unnecessary risks." This was concrete proof that while Aegis might not exactly be hunting down motorcycle riders, they certainly were not programmed to avoid them.

Wow. Read this," Jack said to Slim, sliding over the papers opened to the road safety page.

"What am I looking for?" asked Slim.

"Just read," instructed Jack.

Jack watched Slim skim through the text.

"Oh shit. Oh shit," he kept saying as his brain processed what the secret files were confirming.

"Yeah, crazy," said Jack. "The question is, what do we do with this information?"

"We go to the police with it?" suggested Leah.

"True, we could. But a lot of times, whistleblowers just go missing," said Jack. "I don't really know you that well, but I am guessing you don't want to end up dead."

"Oh god no," said Leah with a shudder. "So what do we do then?"

"Hmm. You make copies. We mail them to all the major news networks?" suggested Jack.

Slim was deep in thought. "Not a bad idea, but that could take weeks for the press to validate it and act upon it. In the meantime, our guys keep dying."

"Yeah, good point," said Jack. "Maybe we let our club brothers know to stay off their bikes until we take down these bastards?"

"Take down?" asked Leah.

"Yeah. Like sabotage their control centers and hobble their fleet of killer cars?" said Slim.

"Whoo," Leah inhaled. "That's dangerous."

"Well, you just told us these cars are programmed to kill. That's not dangerous?" asked Slim.

"Slim's right," said Jack. "We have to do something. We can't wait for the press to get all this info, fact-check it, then release it. That could be weeks."

"Well, maybe don't ride your motorcycles until then?" suggested Leah.

Jack and Slim looked at each other in silence. After about forty-five seconds, they both burst into hysterical laughter.

"Yeah, right," said Slim. "Like that would happen."

"Ugh. I guess you're right," Leah replied. "I could tell you where their main control center is, but security is tight."

"That would help. Thanks, Leah," said Jack.

"What are you going to do? Blow it up?" she asked.

"Hmm, not a bad idea, but that could kill some innocent workers," said Jack. "That's not really my style."

"Well, what then?" asked Leah.

"What about pranks?" suggested Slim.

"Pranks?" said Leah.

"Yeah. Like mail them an envelope of a 'white powder', could be cocaine, say, but they think it's anthrax; they will have to shut down the office for a day or so. Phone in a bomb threat after that. You know, just keep messing with them."

"That could work," shrugged Leah.

"We also need to think about all the Aegis cars on the road, too," said Jack. "I'm sure those could monitor us, right?"

Leah thought for a moment. "Yeah, they probably could."

"Speaking of. Now that I know all this, I don't think it's safe for you to go home," said Jack.

"What? Where am I meant to go?" asked Leah.

"She could stay at my place," suggested Slim.

Jack could already tell that Leah did not look happy about the idea.

"No offense, bud, but a young lady like this isn't going to feel comfortable staying at some dude's place she barely knows," said Jack.

"Ah, right," said Slim, looking crestfallen.

"I have an idea," said Jack. "She could stay at your place, and you could crash at mine. Your place is pretty out of the way. She would be safe there."

"Yeah, we could do that," said Slim.

"Hold up. I have no change of clothes, no toiletries. I need to go back and grab some stuff," said Leah.

"No way," said Jack. "We have to assume by now they are watching your place. Actually, thinking about it, pop your SIM card from your cell phone too."

Leah had a look on her face like she hadn't thought of that. She grabbed her iPhone and popped the SIM card out.

"Look, there is a big Walmart out near Slim's place. We can all head out there, get you a change of clothes, some toiletries, and maybe a cheap pay-as-you-go cell phone," suggested Jack.

Both Leah and Slim thought about it for a moment. "That could work," Leah finally replied.

"That's settled then," said Jack. "Let's get out of here while there are still tons of traffic on the roads. Harder to spot us."

Chapter Nine

They made it to the Walmart near Slim's, where Jack gave Leah some money to buy a change of clothes and a burner cell phone. They made the short ride over to Slim's place in Apache Junction and parked in his garage. Jack eyed Slim's truck as they wheeled their bikes inside. No sense in leaving their scoots out in the open. For all he knew, Aegis could have airborne drones scouting for them or even access to satellites. They couldn't take any chances at this stage.

Slim grabbed a sports bag and stuffed it full of some fresh socks and underwear, a couple of T-shirts, and another pair of jeans. He then ran to his bathroom, grabbed his toothbrush, toothpaste, and shaving kit.

"Okay, I'm ready," he declared.

"Well, hold up. Let's let Leah get settled first," said Jack.

"Shit, yeah. You're right," Slim replied. Slim showed her the bedroom and bathroom, where he kept fresh bed sheets and towels. He showed her how to operate the TV and then gave her his Wi-Fi password.

"Safe to say," said Jack, "do not try to log onto the Aegis website in any way, shape, or form. You'll be alerting them to your location immediately."

"Oh, don't worry. I have no intention of that," Leah replied.

"We should give you our numbers," suggested Slim. "Maybe use a different name when texting us, too. You know, just in case they are monitoring texts."

"Yeah, good thinking," said Leah. Knowing what she knew about Aegis, she didn't think they could access people's private text messages, but then again, she didn't think they would program their cars to kill bikers either.

"If you get bored, perhaps start building a list of investigative journalists who would be into covering this," suggested Jack.

"Yeah, I was already planning on it," said Leah, giving him a thumbs-up gesture.

The two bikers were getting ready to leave Leah at Slim's house.

"Hey Slim, I've been thinking," said Jack.

"What's that?" Slim replied.

"It might pay to leave our bikes here and take your truck," said Jack.

"Yeah, I get ya," said Slim. "We can do that."

"Nice," said Jack. "Hey Leah, I live not far from here, East Mesa. We'll be back in the morning to get you breakfast and figure out our next moves."

"You gonna be okay?" asked Slim.

"Yeah, I think so. Thanks for everything," said Leah, watching the pair back out of Slim's garage. As she watched them leave, her mind was going a thousand miles an hour. This is nuts, she thought. I'm on the run from an extremely powerful tech company and staying at a biker's house that I only met two hours ago. She did realize, though, that if she hadn't stumbled upon Jack and Slim, she would probably be dead by now. She shuddered and locked Slim's front door.

Chapter Ten

The next day, Jack took Leah to a local copy shop, where she ran off various extra sets of her incriminating documents. Using the info she had sourced the night before, she mailed out packets to a bunch of hard-nosed "investigative journalists." The remainder of the names on her list, she could email a file folder to from a disposable Gmail account she had set up. After she had finished all her work at the copy shop, Jack took her to a supermarket to pick up more food for her stay and then dropped her off at home.

After that, he returned to his place. It wouldn't do Leah any good to be spotted by Aegis goons before her story got leaked to the press. With stage one of their plan in motion, Jack decided to reach out to the remaining Desert Saints Motorcycle Club for an emergency meeting. He didn't want to hold it at their clubhouse, as he was sure it was being watched either by law enforcement or Aegis security personnel.

After a flurry of text messages and phone calls, it was settled that they would meet at a nondescript sports bar on the far edge of Eastern Mesa (next stop the desert). Jack advised no one to fly their colors and to ride in their personal vehicles, leaving their motorcycles at home.

Jack and Slim pulled up at seven-thirty in the evening and sat in the car park for the next fifteen minutes, watching the area before they even got out of Slim's truck. Tensions were running high, and they didn't want to risk walking into an ambush or being caught in the middle of a stakeout. Considering it was a Thursday night, the sports bar was pretty deserted. Confident that there was no sinister force watching them in the shadows, Jack decided he would get out, scope the car park and the surrounding area, then go inside and do the same before the rest of the club showed up. At least if he got arrested or "taken away," the rest of the club could carry out their plans without him.

Jack walked a circuit of the car park and checked out the neighboring businesses, too, just in case law enforcement had set up a surveillance van outside of the bar's car park. Nothing. Satisfied there was no "spy van" nearby, he walked past Slim's truck, gave him a nod, and headed into the back entrance of the sports bar. He had drunk there a couple of times in the past, but it was hardly what he considered a local watering hole, preferring the biker bars in Sunnyslope and Cave Creek.

He walked in, scoping the bar out as he went. There were a couple of old geezers in a booth; no way were they cops. At the bar, there were two older women who had seen better days. Too many parties, too many smokes, too much booze, they were probably only mid-50s, but they were sitting there looking like they were seventy-five years each. Ouch.

Pleased that the place wasn't swarming with snitches, he exited the bar and gave Slim the thumbs up. Slim popped out of his truck, locked it, and walked up to Jack.

"All good, brother?" he asked.

"Well, unless they have a spy satellite hovering above us, I think we're going to be alright," said Jack.

"Okay, cool. I'll text the boys the green light," said Slim, whipping out his cell phone.

"Let's go grab a beer," said Jack.

"Or two," joked Slim as they headed back inside.

Chapter Eleven

Within the hour, the rest of the Desert Saints arrived at the sports bar. Shorty and Tex from Slim's brother's funeral were there along with six other club brothers. Everyone grabbed beers, and they pushed two tables near the back of the bar (and away from the front windows) together to accommodate everyone.

'So what's the emergency meeting all about?" asked Tex.

"Aegans," said Slim.

"What's that?" asked Mike, one of the Desert Saints from Goodyear.

"Those self-driving cars, bro. Like Uber with no driver," explained Shorty.

"No shit. They have those now?" asked Mike.

"Yeah," said Shorty.

"So what about them?" asked Mike.

Jack sighed. It was going to be a long night.

"Well. Basically, we have been talking to this chick from the company that makes them. She has proof that these cars are programmed to kill bikers."

"Get the fuck out," said three of the guys at the same time.

"Are you serious?" asked Tex.

'Deadly. She has the REAL stats to prove it. We spent the morning mailing out to every investigative journalist in the nation an information packet to bring these fuckers down," said Jack.

"Wow," said Shorty, "So what do you need us to do, bro?"

"We need to stop 'em," said Slim.

"What about these reporters?" asked Goodyear Mike.

'That could take some time, bro," said Jack. "We need to stay alive until then. Actually, not just us, all riders in the Phoenix Metro"

'Oh boy," said Mike, "What ya got in mind?"

"What we have always done," stated Slim.

"What's that?" asked Goodyear Mike.

'We fight back,' said Slim with determination, 'We hit 'em hard"

"How, though?" asked Mike.

'Old school," said Jack

"What's that mean?' asked Tex.

'Fire bombs bro. Molotov cocktails," said Jack.

"We could find their depot and take out as many as possible," suggested Slim.

"That's good," said Jack, "I was thinking more like we bait them out."

'What do you mean?" asked Shorty.

"We split into teams. 1 rider and 2 dudes in a car. One drives, one has a stack of liquor bottles, and when an Aegis starts running down one of our guys on his Harley, the other two will take out the car."

"Ohh, that's good," said Tex. "I wanna be one of the bait guys"

'Right on," said Shorty.

"We should start Sunday night. Too many people on the roads on Friday and Saturday nights. We want to take out the bad guys, not innocent folks, ya know?" suggested Jack.

"Yeah. I like the way you think," said Mike.

"Let's split into teams and figure out a battle plan," said Slim.

'Right on, boys," said Tex. Raising his beer glass to his club brothers.

Chapter Twelve

The Desert Saints spent the next week carrying out their war of terror on the self-driving cars of Phoenix.

After a couple of attempts, they fine-tuned their art of destruction. In each of the three groups of club brothers, one of them would ride a planned-out stretch of one of the many freeways on their motorcycle. As soon as they spotted an Aegis self-driving car with no passenger on board, the two Desert Saints in a vehicle would pull alongside and lob a Molotov cocktail onto the driverless vehicle, immediately setting it on fire. Then the car would be forced to pull to the side of the road, per its programming, and sit by the side of the road as it burned to a cinder.

Jack had to admit it was a satisfying feeling seeing these murderous cars go up in flames. Screw them and screw their founder, Mr Bishop.

Shorty and Tex got lucky. They were in a section of uptown Phoenix called the Coronado and found three separate Aegis all idling together. With two Molotov cocktails, they took out three vehicles.

Jack monitored the media every night. Still no media coverage. Still no outrage. What was taking them so long? He assumed fact-checking. That was the best-case scenario. Worst-case scenario, Aegis president and founder, Mr. Bishop, had enough power and sway to silence the media. If that was indeed true, they had a bigger fight than they had initially anticipated. As he had done for most of his life, Jack hoped for the best but prepared for the worst-case scenario.

The club continued to meet in random bars and coffee shops in Eastern Mesa. Jack was pleased to see that despite the dangers, all the club brothers actually enjoyed their "missions." The chance to destroy someone else's expensive property in the name of "truth and justice" was an opportunity too good to pass up. Most of the guys had been hooligans and troublemakers in their teenage years, but work and family responsibilities, plus the fear of serious jail time, had curbed those destructive impulses. To get to act like a teenager again in the name of biker survival was too good to be true.

Jack was driving Leah nuts, bugging her every couple of days to see how she was progressing with the investigative reporters. She was doing follow-up emails and calls, but so far the silence had been deafening.

The following Wednesday, the club met at a bowling alley. As per his normal behavior, Slim and Jack got there thirty minutes earlier and checked out their surroundings before giving the boys the heads-up that it was safe to arrive. So far, they had been lucky but also clever. They had set out to never strike in the same location twice and to vary their attacks so they didn't leave an obvious pattern. Jack recalled reading somewhere that many serial killers struck in the same area, time and time again, because that was a neighborhood they were familiar with. He knew dealing with a big-brain "genius" like Mr Bishop from the Aegean corporation, and suspected a guy like that would be looking for pattern recognition to try and establish who was attacking his prized and expensive vehicles.

Slim sent a group text to everyone advising them that the coast was clear, and Jack and Slim went inside. The bowling alley was loud and noisy, but thankfully not crowded. The patrons were either teens or families, and, unless law enforcement was conducting a stakeout with their kids, Jack was confident they would be okay.

By 8 p.m., all the Desert Saints were there but Tex, Mike, and Shorty. Concerned, Jack had any of the boys who were close to the guys call them. No answer from Tex and Mike, but Shorty didn't pick up; he did text back, "Be there in fifteen."

Jack breathed a sigh of relief, so they were just running late. It happens. This part of Eastern Mesa was a good 25-minute ride from the Tempe side. People had no clue how big Mesa really was.

Finally, Shorty arrived. He had a bandage on his left arm and a field dressing on his right temple.

"What the hell happened to you?" asked Slim.

Shorty looked like he was fighting back tears.

"Tex and Mike are dead, man."

"WHAT?" said everyone at the table in unison.

"Dude. What the hell?" asked Jack.

"Ugh, fuck. Last night," winced Shorty, who seemed in a lot of pain. "We were out hunting robot cars."

"We all were," said one of the Desert Saints at their table.

"We were on the I-10 heading west," Shorty continued. "We saw an Aegis car, so Mike rode ahead as bait. You know, like we had been doing."

"Yeah," said Jack, visualizing the scenario in his head as Shorty talked.

"The fucking thing attacked him, like accelerated and ran him down. Tex rammed the car to get him off poor Mike, but it was too late."

Half the guys swore under their breath.

"But what happened to Tex?" asked Slim.

"Yeah. So that's the crazy thing," Shorty replied. "Two more Aegis cars appeared out of nowhere, like they had been trailing that car."

"What?" asked Jack.

"Like they were using the first car as bait," explained Shorty.

"Wow," said Slim.

"One of the cars rammed us. Tex backed up, and we tried to get out of there," Shorty continued. "The two Aegis cars gave chase. We tried to get away. Have you ever seen those videos of the police doing the PIT maneuver?"

Slim looked at Jack. "You mean they come up to the rear wheel well and turn into it?"

"Yes! Exactly like that," said Shorty. "They flipped our vehicle, and it rolled over a couple of times."

"What the fuck!" said Jack.

"That's what I said," Shorty replied. "I got thrown out, and Tex was trapped in the vehicle."

"Damn," said Slim.

"By the time I came to my senses, our car was on fire," Shorty explained. "One of the two Aegis came after me. I had to leap over the highway divide to avoid it."

"Fuck," said one of the Desert Saints.

"I just hoped Tex was dead before our car caught fire," said Shorty. "Getting burnt alive is no way to go."

"Hell no," shuddered Slim.

"So the cars are actively coming after us now?" said Jack.

"Yeah, seems that way," said Shorty.

"Well, this changes everything," said Slim.

"I'm going to talk to Leah in the morning and find out what we can do," said Jack.

"I tell you what we need to do," said Slim. "We need to hit 'em where it hurts."

"Yeah," said one of the guys. "We need revenge."

"No one touches our brothers and gets away with it," said another of the Desert Saints. "You mess with one of us, you mess with all of us."

"Damn right," said Shorty.

"Okay. Let's not rush into anything. Let's formulate a plan and hit 'em hard," said Jack. "This is straight-up murder. They take out two of our guys. I say we take out their entire fleet."

"Yeah. But what do we have?" asked Slim. "Shorty ain't in good shape. That pretty much leaves six of us to take them all on."

"Well, we can't outnumber them, so we have to resort to guerrilla-style tactics," said Jack. "Let me sleep on it and come up with a plan. I would say until then, no one rode their Harley. Stick to four wheels. Got it?"

Chapter Thirteen

The next morning, Slim and Jack drove over to his house to meet with Leah. First, they took her grocery shopping, then they grabbed coffee.

"So I have news for you guys," said Leah. "Two different reporters have gotten back to me asking more questions."

"Just two from that massive list?" asked Slim.

"Well, two is a start," Leah replied. "A good start."

"True," said Jack. "Hey, I gotta ask you something."

"What's that?" asked Leah.

"Two of our guys were killed by Aegis the other night on the I-10," said Jack.

"Oh no. I'm so sorry," said Leah.

"Well, here's the kicker," Jack continued. "They rammed one of the Aegis cars, and two more willfully attacked them, like they were lying in wait."

"What??" said Leah. "That goes against all their programming."

"Well, it happened," said Jack.

Leah thought for a moment. "It has to be someone super high up. Any basic Aegean programmer has to have their work reviewed by at least three different departments, for obvious reasons. It MUST be someone way, way up the chain of command at Aegis Mobility."

"Any idea who?" asked Jack.

"Not off the top of my head," Leah replied. "Give me some time to try and figure it out."

"Well, we don't have time. Two of my guys died the other night. I have to do something NOW," said Jack.

"I get that," said Leah.

"What can you tell me about the depot? Like, where is it located? How many cars would be there?" asked Jack.

Leah thought for a second. "The main depot is out in that new industrial park near Goodyear. Do you know it?"

Jack thought for a moment. "Is it near that new Amazon fulfillment center?" he asked.

"Kinda," said Leah. "I can draw you a map."

"Thanks, Leah. How many vehicles would you say are on the premises?" asked Jack.

"Hmm. I would guess two hundred to two fifty?" Leah replied.

"Please draw me a map," asked Jack.

Leah got up and walked over to the counter of the coffee shop. She returned with a notepad and a pen. After a few minutes of quick doodling, she sketched out the layout of the Aegean car depot, which she handed to Jack.

The biker examined the map and asked a couple of questions for clarification. Satisfied he had the general layout figured out, he and Slim drove Leah back to Slim's place. They said their goodbyes and returned to Jack's place.

"Well? What do you think?" asked Slim on the ride back to Jack's.

"I've got a plan," said Jack.

"Of course you do," Slim replied.

Chapter Fourteen

The bikers monitored the news stations for the next few days leading into the weekend. Still no exposé on the corrupt and evil Aegis corporation. What the hell? They did see a news piece on the local news about the death of Tex and Mike. To the bikers' shock, the mainstream media was implying that the crash was between Mike and Tex. No mention of the self-driving cars' involvement whatsoever.

Sunday evening was "go time." Jack had a basic plan. He figured their best bet was to keep everything as simple as possible. No storming the car yard with armed men and getting into a violent shootout with Aegis security and local law enforcement. That would be a fight they would never win. Stealth would be the order of the day. They were outnumbered and outgunned; all they could do was fight dirty if they wanted to win this.

Jack had borrowed Tucson Tim's Chevy van. He took with him Slim and Frank from Yavapai County. In the back of the van, they had two five-gallon tanks of gas. There was a trap door at the bottom of Tim's van. That's where the fun would begin.

They cruised up the I-10 West until they found the turnoff Leah had mapped out for them. Two blocks from the Aegis car depot, they pulled over. Frank jumped out and put a bunch of magnets on Tim's rear license plate to avoid any license-plate-reading software.

Jack pulled on a full-face motorcycle helmet. You know, just in case the perimeter had facial-recognition software on its security cameras. Slim pulled on a plain black hoodie, a dark baseball cap, and a disposable surgeon's face mask. Satisfied they were ready, Jack drove the last 2 blocks in silence. Everyone knew their roles to play.

There it was: the Aegis depot. There was a front office about half a city block long with a service road down the side. From Leah's description, the service road ran along either side of the building, and parallel to the street was an alleyway that ran all the way to the end of the block.

Jack signaled a right turn and cruised down the side service road. On his verbal command, Frank popped the trap door in the bottom of Tim's van. Then he grabbed a hose, put it into the top of one of the gas cans, and sucked until the gas started rising. He threaded the hose out the trap door and aimed it toward the chain-link fence on the left side of the Aegis car park. Gasoline ran out along the perimeter of the fence line as Jack drove very slowly up toward the back alley. Anyone watching from a security camera would not be able to spot the trickle of gas running into the car park.

Jack reached the back alley that ran parallel to the street and turned right, keeping the van rolling at a slow, steady pace. By now, he was convinced that every camera in the place was watching them, but it was too bad. He was on a mission.

"You ready?" he asked Slim.

"Yep," Slim replied.

"Remember, run to the end of the alley. We will be there waiting for you," said Jack.

"I know," said Slim, fixing his face mask.

As the Chevy van cruised toward the far edge of the Aegis car park, Slim grabbed his backpack filled with road flares and readied himself to exit the vehicle.

Jack said quietly, "Okay, bro," and Slim popped the back door and slipped into the darkness. Frank pulled it shut, and Jack continued his tour of the outskirts of the building. He turned right at the corner, so he was now running parallel to the other side of the building, heading back toward the street.

Frank told him to slow down as he changed out the gas cans and did the same trick to siphon gas out. The whole back of the van reeked of gasoline, but that was to be expected.

They continued until they reached the edge of the car park, but before the administration building. Jack wanted the cars gone, but had no intention of burning up any workers inside on the overnight shift. They were just pawns in all of this, and chances are, most of the workers were totally unaware of the homicidal programming the driverless cars had in them.

They reached the road, and Jack signaled left to head down the block. As he was looking both ways for traffic, he saw two security guards exit the front of the building and head toward them. Too late, fellas, we are gone.

They drove back down the block away from the Aegean building. Reaching the next corner, Jack turned left and cruised up the street, trying to find a suitable spot to pull over and wait for Slim. He swung a sneaky U-turn and parked up right near the alley. They had to be ready for Slim to make a quick getaway. He would be coming in hot after he tossed his road flares into the car park.

Jack pulled off the helmet and threw it into the back of the van. While he was doing that, Frank closed up the trap door and popped the lid back on the half-filled gas can.

"You good?" asked Jack.

"Yeah. You?" said Frank.

"You know it."

"How will we know if Slim succeeds?" asked Frank.

"I'm sure we will know," smiled Jack.

Jack could hear footfalls as someone approached down the alley. It had to be Slim.

"Go. Go. Go. Go," said Slim as he came running up. He wrenched open the sliding side door, jumped in, and slammed it shut. "Go," he said again.

Jack didn't hesitate. He took off fast but smoothly. No way was he trying to draw any attention to himself as they fled the scene of the crime.

Just as they reached the street corner that led to Aegis's vehicle depot, they heard a massive explosion. Seemed like some of the cars had caught fire. Those lithium batteries, I never trusted those, thought Jack as they rolled away from the scene of the crime. They had crossed the block when they heard yet another, more thunderous explosion. It rattled the van windows; it was so loud. Multiple alarms started blaring. It would probably only be a minute or two more before the entire area was shut down with law enforcement and the fire department. They had to fast-track it to the freeway home immediately.

As Jack found the on-ramp for the eastbound interstate, a steady stream of cop cars and fire trucks was heading the other way. He was sure that Tim's van would show up on the security cameras. Other than the make and model, they would come up with nothing. Tim basically used the van only for collector car shows; it was not his daily driver or anything, so he felt confident nothing would be linked back to Tim or the club.

They dropped off Frank at his girlfriend's place in Tempe and drove back to Tim's storage facility. There, they would lock the van up and take Slim's truck back to Jack's place.

"You reckon this might hit the news?" asked Slim as they rode back from the storage garage.

"Well, guys like Mr. Bishop from Aegis Corp pay to keep themselves out of the media as much as in the media. So who knows? Maybe," said Jack.

"Yeah. I'm thinking the same," Slim replied.

They parked Slim's vehicle in Jack's garage and headed inside. Despite it being 4 a.m. and being totally exhausted, Jack wanted a cold beer and to check out the TV news. He grabbed one for Slim as well.

They put their feet up, and Jack hit the TV's remote. They flicked through the channels until they found an early morning news network. There it was.

"Terrorists attack tech company" was how the media was pitching it. Helicopter footage of the depot looked like a war zone. Jack wondered if even the admin building was still standing.

At least no one was killed, from what the news anchor was saying. The FBI had been informed. No mention of Tim's van. Did the fires destroy the security tapes? No chance. Jack imagined a company like that would have a feed to other data centers. Backups upon backups of all data were how places like that worked.

"Wow. We did it," said Slim, taking in the news coverage. "You think we got 'em all?"

"I doubt it. But we have had to hurt them. Big time," said Jack.

"Yeah. I think I read somewhere those cars are worth like $200,000 each," said Slim.

"Oh, I'm sure," Jack replied. "Got to be at least a twenty-million dollar loss right there."

"Easily," Slim replied.

Jack finished his beer and went to bed. Slim stayed up watching a little more TV before crashing out on Jack's couch.

It was after 10 a.m. when Jack finally woke up. He was still tired. He grabbed his phone and saw there was a message from Leah. It was vague, just as they had prearranged, just in case someone at Aegis had a way of analyzing text messages. Could not be too careful with these tech nerds.

Jack made a pot of coffee as he waited for Slim to wake up. He texted Leah back and said they would meet her for lunch at Slim's place around 2 p.m.

The aroma of fresh coffee finally woke Slim around 11 a.m. He staggered through to the kitchen.

"Morning, bro. Get any sleep?" he asked.

"Yeah, a bit. Kinda exhausted to be honest," said Slim.

"Yeah, me too. There's fresh coffee in the pot. We gotta go meet Leah in a few, so shower up and be ready to roll in 90 minutes, okay?"

"Okay, roger that," said Slim, making a beeline for the coffee pot.

Chapter Fifteen

Jack and Slim cruised over to Slim's place to pick up Leah that afternoon.

"What news do you think she's got for us?" asked Slim.

"I dunno, man. Hopefully something about the news investigation," said Jack.

"Yeah, man. I need to ride my bike. You know," said Slim.

"Yeah, me too, bro. Me too," said Jack.

Slim ran in to collect Leah while Jack sat and waited behind the wheel of Slim's vehicle. Slim was good like that, happy to lend a brother his car at a moment's notice or just let you drive it while he traveled shotgun. He was an easy guy to like, thought Jack.

Leah came out of Slim's place and gave Jack a small wave when she saw him behind the wheel. Slim let her take the passenger seat, and he climbed in the back. Satisfied everyone was in safely, Jack put the car in drive and cruised to the local strip mall. There, he found a small mom-and-pop burger joint that seemed worthy of checking out. At some of these small places, a burger, fries, and a soda cost the same as they would from one of the big-time fast-food places, but the quality was ten times superior.

After ordering, they gathered around a small table at the back of the hole-in-the-wall burger joint.

"So what news do you have for us?" asked Jack.

"Actually, I have some great news," said Leah with a big smile on her face. "Sally Fisker-Murphy from the Action News Nation TV network has her story ready to go."

"Whoa," said Slim. "She's pretty good."

"Ready to go? What does that mean?" asked Jack.

"Well, it means she did her research, shot a segment, and it's ready to air," explained Leah. "I guess it's a matter of the network clearing everything with their legal team and then setting up a broadcast date."

"Hmm, so it could be weeks away?" asked Jack.

"No, not at all," said Leah. "Because of your 'terrorist' attack on Aegean Corporation, media interest is very high. For a network to come out now with another side to the story is very timely; they need this to air in the next 48 hours to get maximum ratings."

This was good news. Ultimately, however, Jack was disappointed that it took them risking life and limb with their firebombing to get anyone to take note of their plight in Phoenix. If they hadn't run their saboteur mission Sunday night, would these people even care?

"Wow, that's great," said Slim.

"Oh yeah. Check this out. Sally's team actually got two more whistleblowers from Aegean to speak out. I think if it had just been me, they would have been much more skeptical. With two others pretty much backing up what I said, it makes it much more legit."

"Wow, that's great," said Jack. Maybe the tide really was turning in their favor.

Chapter Sixteen

The following Monday, Jack and Slim returned from work when Jack's phone went off. He grabbed it and checked the screen. It was from Leah: "7 pm A.N.N."

"Who is it, bro?" asked Slim.

"Holy shit! I think it's happening," said Jack.

"What?" asked Slim.

"The news story. Leah says 7 pm tonight." Jack checked the clock on his microwave. It was 6:55 pm.

"C'mon, we just about have time," said Jack.

He went to the fridge, grabbed two beers, and pulled out a huge bag of chips from one of his kitchen cupboards. He rummaged around in another cupboard before retrieving a popcorn bucket. That would do. He poured the chips into the large bucket and headed into the living room.

Slim was already on the couch, remote in hand, trying to find the Action News Nation channel.

"I think you passed it, bro," said Jack, realizing that Slim was now in the movie part of the channel listings. Slim went back instead of forward with the remote. Finally, he found A.N.N.

They cracked their beers and munched on potato chips as the news anchors started their broadcast. Typical of these news shows, they teased the big story but made you watch a bunch of other stories first to keep you locked into the channel.

Then finally, there it was. The big expose. Aegean Corporation had knowingly put code into their self-driving cars to wipe out bikers. The spokesman for Mr. Bishop was flustered and skirted around the facts when put on the spot. The news business was a twisted business that loved to sensationalize any negative story on bike clubs, so it was nice to see a network that actually showed sympathy toward bikers.

The following week was a whirlwind of craziness. As expected, other news outlets picked up on the story, and it gained momentum. Leah had built the foundation by getting her original information out to as many reporters as possible. Once they saw what was going on, they all fell in line and released their own stories. There was no escaping it.

To add insult to injury, Aegean Corp founder Mr. Bishop was arrested on the tarmac at a private airport in Scottsdale as he was planning to make a break for South America. Under heavy questioning and faced with so much evidence of wrongdoing, the tech "genius" finally cracked and confessed to multiple charges of vehicular homicide.

Aegis vehicles were recalled from the roads, and it was back to Ubers and Lyft cars all over again.

Soon, the Desert Saints were back on the roads, safe in the knowledge that homicidal robot cars were off the streets. It was hard enough in this day and age to ride safely with everyone glued to their phones, texting at 60 mph as it was.

The final nail in the coffin for Mr. Bishop was a follow-up interview from prison, where he let his public face slip and admitted that he programmed his cars to take out "Scooter Trash" (his words) because a biker had stolen the man's first girlfriend back in college. All this over a broken heart? Figures, scoffed Jack as he rode off on two wheels once more.

The Long Silence

The prison gates of Florence creaked open, and Dane Maddox stepped out into the sunlight he hadn't felt on his face in twenty years. He was older, harder. His beard was white now, his tattoos faded to blue-green ghosts.

The warden asked if anyone was coming for him. Dane shook his head. The Diablo Sons Motorcycle Club was long gone, scattered, dead, or rotting behind bars. He had no patch, no brothers, no reason to ride back into towns that had forgotten him.

Instead, he bought a beat-up pickup with the little cash he'd scraped together from prison jobs and drove until pavement gave way to dirt, until even the buzz of power lines vanished and the only sound was the wind pushing sand across the desert floor.

That's where he built his place, a trailer, sunbaked and rusted, dropped in the middle of nowhere. A steel water tank. A fire pit out front. An old Harley he'd found at an auction, half buried in dust, sitting like a monument to a life that used to matter.

Nights were the hardest. He'd sit outside with a cigarette, watching stars burn holes in the black sky. Coyotes yipped in the distance. Sometimes he thought he heard the low growl of Harleys coming over the horizon, the ghost of his old brothers riding for him. But it was just the wind.

Days stretched long and quiet. He worked on his bike, rode the dirt trails when the sun wasn't too brutal, then came back to silence. The desert didn't ask questions. Didn't care what he'd done. It was the first place that.

Give him peace instead of blood.

But the past had a way of crawling out of the grave.

One afternoon, a black SUV appeared on the dirt road, kicking up a snake of dust. A young man in a crisp suit stepped out, sweating in the heat. "You, Dane Maddox?" he asked.

Dane didn't answer. He just lit another smoke.

The kid licked his lips. "My father rode with the Diablo Sons. Said if I ever found you, I should tell you he went down clean. Said you'd understand." He placed a patch, frayed, sun-faded, on the hood of the truck.

Dane stared at it for a long time, the old skull and wings emblem staring back. His chest ached with something he thought the years had burned out of him.

The kid finally left. Dane didn't stop him.

That night, Dane poured a bottle of cheap whiskey on the desert floor, lit a fire, and sat beside his bike. He didn't say a word, but in the silence he felt them all again, their laughter, their rage, the thunder of a hundred engines rolling down I-10.

For the first time in twenty years, he smiled.

The desert had given him solitude. But it had also given him back his ghosts. And he figured that was enough.

One Hour to Die

Chapter One

Biker Andy Harlan was heading home. Growing up in the northern Arizona town of Blackwood Ridge, Andy couldn't wait to leave. It was small, everyone knew everyone, and nothing exciting ever happened there. Even the closest town, Sedona, was boring. Back then, he had yearned for action and adventure. Phoenix was the nearest major city. Maybe there or Los Angeles was his goal as a teenager. Slayer, Metallica. Those bands had played Phoenix. They would never play Sedona; they would never play Blackwood Ridge.

All they had to do as kids was ride their dirt bikes around. They knew every canyon, every mountain, every riverbed in their county. It was fun, but it wasn't enough. As soon as he graduated from high school, he moved to Phoenix with his best buddy Steve. They got a cheap apartment and jobs at a local pizza place. He learned to make pizzas, and they both put in the hours. Even with all that work, they barely scraped by. At least they didn't have to pay for food; they had all the free pizza they could want.

As soon as they could, Steve and Andy bought used Honda Shadow motorcycles. Hondas were tough machines; they could take a lot of abuse, but you still had to service them. Neither of the guys could afford to take the bikes to a shop, so they learned to wrench on their machines themselves, something Andy found he grew to enjoy. Those early days were a blast: work all the time, ride their bikes in their free time, catch rock and metal shows when they came to town.

Like all good things, they eventually had to come to an end. Steve got his girlfriend pregnant and announced he was quitting the pizza joint to sign up for the Navy. Andy didn't hesitate and signed up too. He always wanted to see the world, and what better way to do so than to have Uncle Sam pay for it?

Basic training was a blast. Some dudes hated it, but you got to work out, eat well, and get paid to learn basic weapon-handling skills. Andy and Steve were in heaven. After basic training, he was selected to be trained as a machinist for a destroyer. Part of his job was to be able to fabricate and replace any moving part for the entire ship. Let's face it: if a part broke down or wore out three months out to sea, you couldn't just swing by the local AutoZone or Lowe's and pick up a replacement part, could you? It was Andy's job to make a new one. He loved it.

Being part of the US Navy, Andy got to travel all over the world: Norway, the United Kingdom, the Middle East, Australia, and even Antarctica. Places he never dreamt he would ever see in a million years. The funny thing was, the more he traveled the world and saw all of these exotic places, the more he realized how special his hometown of Blackwood Ridge really was.

In time, his mother passed. He never really knew his dad. His dad had been killed in a car accident when he was two years old. His mother did the best she could raising him and his big sister, but as soon as he left home, his communication with them both was minimal. In time, his sister married and moved to Oregon. He probably hears from her twice a year these days.

Five years into his enlistment, Steve was killed. Not during any act of war, but something closer to home. He had been living off base and had started seeing a lady he wanted to marry, long after he had broken up with the mother of his child. The new woman's jealous ex-boyfriend couldn't take rejection and shot them both. That loss hurt as much as losing his mother. Steve was the closest thing Andy had to a brother, and now he was gone. They say loss like that is healed by time. Andy disagreed. He just became numb. If he let himself feel it, he would not be able to function.

After eight years of service, Andy left the Navy. First, he got work in a San Diego custom car shop, doing fabrication, making replacement panels for older model cars, and stuff like that. After a year at that shop, he felt he had to leave San Diego and move back to Arizona. Being around boats, open water, and harbors was still too painful for him. Maybe one day, but not anytime in the near future.

Andy quickly got a job at one of the top hot rod and custom car joints in Mesa. It felt good to be back in the desert heat and dry air compared to the moderate Mediterranean climate of San Diego. He did everything you were meant to do: he got married, bought a house, and had kids. Twenty years later, he got divorced, lost his house, and rarely saw his kids. His ex-wife had poisoned them against him. From what he heard talking to other bikers all over the greater Phoenix metro area, he wasn't alone.

To deal with the impact of his divorce, Andy had thrown himself headlong into his work. He had worked pretty much every day for the last years without a break, including weekends. He was beyond burnt out. His boss insisted he take some time off. At a loss on what to do, he decided to return home to Blackwood Ridge, check out the house he grew up in, see if any of his old school friends were still in town, stuff like that.

He would book himself a motel room on the outskirts of town. He would ride his motorcycle up, stay a week, and try to forget about all the chaos in his life. Relax, unwind, and recharge. Just what the doctor ordered.

Chapter Two

Andy always had an impending sense of doom whenever he took time off work. Like the moment he would step away from the grind, a runaway 18-wheeler would plow through a red light and wipe him out or something. No real logic to it, just a feeling. Leaving his rented apartment and rolling through the mid-morning streets of Phoenix, he felt the same. He shrugged it off; after all, he felt this way anytime he had a vacation.

The ride home to Blackwood Ridge was an easy one. Straight up the I-17 Interstate, take a left at Sedona, and keep rolling. It should be a little over two hours of riding time on his Harley. Once he climbed up and out of the valley, he started to relax. A simple case of paranoia, just like every other time.

The open plains above Phoenix always blew his mind. It was like he was in Iowa or somewhere. You would not know just a few miles below, down in the valley, there was a sprawling metropolis. He enjoyed the solitude and the peace of the open road.

He stopped just before Prescott for a piss break, to top up his gas tank, and grab a cup of coffee. He stretched his legs and rubbed his lower back to get his circulation going again after the hour ride. In the old days, he could ride for hours without issue; these days, anything over a ride to the bar and back wrecked his spine.

Andy finished his coffee, tossed the cup in the trash, and got back on his bike. It should be just under an hour now, and he would be "home." It had been too long. As he continued north on the I-17, he thought of something an old-timer had told him back in San Diego. He was getting tattooed, and his tattooist had been in prison for twenty years back in the day. He said when he got out, he remembered San Diego as it was twenty years ago. All that time he had been behind the wire, the city had moved on. Landmark buildings had been knocked down, replaced by glass and chrome skyscrapers. Fields of crops were now suburban sprawl. Beloved family restaurants were now luxury apartment buildings. The city had moved on. His recollections had not. Andy wondered if this would be the same for him and Blackwood Ridge.

He found the turnoff for Sedona with ease. It was hard to miss. Once a hippy colony, it was now high-end art galleries and gift shops. Not only that, there were places that would do your "chakra readings" and take photos of your "aura." Yeah, right. Nice scam if you can get it, laughed Andy.

He traveled west past Sedona and back on the open roads. Shouldn't be long now. Canyons of red rock everywhere. He hated to admit it to himself, but this was one of the most beautiful places in the entire USA. Nothing else like it. Amazing.

Finally, he started seeing signs for Blackwood Ridge. He was home. It felt weird. Even though he was born and raised here, he almost felt like an outsider in his own town. Funny how being gone so long will do that to a person.

Chapter Three

Andy blipped down through the gears as he reached the outskirts of town. The gas station was still there on his left, just with a revamped facelift that made it look like most modern-day gas stations. Did they have the same dried-up hot dogs that every other station in the USA seemed to have on display (but never sell)?

Andy saw that an old hardware store was now a designer clothing store. As he cruised through town, he spotted an organic supermarket! That would not have lasted one day back in the 1980s. Things sure had changed since he had left town. He shook his head and smiled like an idiot. Civilization had finally come to Blackwood Ridge.

There used to be a cheap motel on the west side of town. Andy wondered if that was now luxury condos or, God forbid, one of those "glamping" sites. Glamorous camping. Who would believe such a thing existed? Go proper old-school camping or go stay at a luxury spa. Don't try to mix the two up. Well, that's at least the way he saw it.

There was definitely a bunch of new construction on Main Street from what he could tell. Did they just keep the facade of the old buildings and build up behind them? He would have to check once he could walk up and down Main Street and not have to keep his eyes on the road.

Finally, reaching the outskirts of town, he saw the ol' reliable "Moto Lodge." It was still there. To tell the truth, he half expected it to be gone, replaced by some hipster-style hotel. He rolled into the forecourt and parked up. Hopefully, they had some rooms available. If not, he was going to have to scramble to find somewhere affordable to sleep.

He spoke to the front desk clerk and was relieved to hear they had some rooms available and they were still under $100. Turns out there were a bunch of "Hipster Hotels" in town, so most visitors avoided the old Moto Lodge. Suited Andy just fine. He imagined those rooms were easily over $300 a night, too. Screw that.

He asked the clerk where the locals drank, and the guy wrote down a couple of names for Andy and a quick explanation on how to find them. Andy grabbed the piece of notebook paper, shoved it into his back pocket, and took the key from the front desk clerk. There were no rooms available on the ground floor of the motel, so Andy was assigned a room on the first floor. He preferred staying on the ground floor so he could wheel his Harley into the room. He would have to have faith that no scumbag would slip onto the property at night and try to steal his beloved ride.

He found his upstairs room with ease and dumped his bag and helmet on the bed. He decided a quick shower was in order to wash off all the road dirt. Refreshed after his shower, he took a little nap and woke up as the sun was setting. At first, he was confused, not quite sure where he was, then it all came back to him. He was home. Andy was hungry and decided to go check out Main Street and see if he could find either of these old dive bars that the locals apparently drank at.

As he was locking his motel room door, he bumped into a businessman, slacks, shirt, and tie, no coat. The man seemed somewhat flustered and was ready to chew Andy out until he saw that Andy was a biker, and just mumbled under his breath and stormed off to his room. Whatever. Andy had run into jerks like that his entire life. Like water off a duck's back, guys like that didn't bother him.

Andy strolled down Main Street. It all felt so surreal to him. Was he home or was he not? There was equally a sense of familiarity and a sense of strangeness to his former hometown. It was very off-putting. The first two food places Andy encountered were no good. One was a high-end steakhouse, and the other was a vegan restaurant! What happened to a good old-fashioned mom-and-pop run burger joint? Did they still exist? Or had the fast-food franchises put them all out of business? He continued heading east.

On the second cross street, Andy spied the first of the locals' preferred dive bars. He made a mental note of where it was and continued his search for food. Finally, he found a small 1950s-style burger joint. He went in, grabbed a stool by the counter, and skimmed the menu. He ended up getting a cheeseburger, fries, and a Coke. If it ain't broke, why try and fix it? The burger was actually pretty decent, real meat, none of this frozen patty nonsense you get at a franchised burger joint. Satisfied with his meal, he paid up and decided to head back to check out the first of these dive bars, the Drunken Ghost.

As expected, the moment he walked in, every head in the place turned to check him out. Ah, small-town living. After sizing him up for a moment, pretty much everyone turned back to whatever they were doing beforehand. He sat at the bar and ordered a beer and a shot of tequila. Two barmaids were working this joint, both pretty girls with a ton of tattoos. He remembered back in the late 1970s, only sailors, bikers, and convicts had tattoos. He wondered when this all changed, the slew of reality tattoo TV shows of the early 2000s, perhaps?

Andy looked around the bar, but he didn't seem to recognize anyone. He hated to admit he was kind of disappointed. But what could he expect? He had moved away. He had left them. He had made no attempt to stay in touch with friends from high school. That was on him and not the people who had stayed behind. Oh well, fuck it. Maybe the other bar was where his old high school pals drank.

He finished his beer and contemplated heading back to the motel. He checked the time. It was nearly 9 pm. In the old days, that would be the time to start properly drinking, not call a time out. He laughed at himself. Getting old sucked. Oh well, one more beer and tequila shot, and he would call it a night.

He raised his hand to the tattooed blonde bartender and pointed at both his beer glass and shot glass. She nodded that she understood and went to pour him more booze. Life wasn't all that bad.

He downed his shot and sipped on his beer. Definitely leaving after this one. Be smart and tap out early.

Andy was halfway through his beer when he felt someone tap him on the shoulder.

"Sorry to interrupt," said the voice.

Andy turned on his barstool to see a man in his mid-50s standing behind him.

"Ah, hello?" said Andy.

"Hey, I'm Dave. Are you Alex Harlan?" asked Dave.

"Alex? No. My name is Andy," said Andy.

"Yeah. Yeah, Andy!" said Dave. "You went to Valley High, didn't ya?"

Andy had gone to Valley High, but for the life of him, he didn't recall this guy going.

"Yeah. I did. Sorry, I don't recall you, Dave. What year did you attend?" asked Andy.

"No, no. My bad," said Dave. "I attended Red Mesa High. We played you guys every year in football."

"Oh shit. No way. That's cool," said Andy. "You live here now?"

"Yeah, moved here twenty years ago. I never see you about town," said Dave.

"I'm just back visiting, would you believe," Andy explained.

"No shit. Very cool. Hey, come grab your drink and sit with us," Dave gestured to a booth with two other guys waving back.

"Sure, why not?" said Andy, grabbing his beer and following Dave over.

Turns out both of Dave's buddies were from Red Mesa, too. When the capitalist hippies all moved to town, they ended up pricing regular folks out. They had all come to Blackwood Ridge as it was still semi-affordable back then. Martin and Jeff were likable dudes too, and before Andy knew it, it was time for last orders, and he was drunker than a skunk.

His new friends vowed to stay in touch with him and made sure he could figure his way back to his motel before they let him leave. Main Street was pretty much deserted at this hour, and as Andy walked home, he smiled to himself. Small-town living was not so bad after all.

Somehow, he navigated his way up the motel stairs to his room. Seems like everyone else in the motel had gone to bed early. Nope, scratch that. As he was unlocking his door, a woman came out of one of the rooms further down the second-floor landing and brushed past him. She seemed in a rush. Whatever.

Andy took a piss, brushed his teeth, and pulled off his boots and jeans. He would shower in the morning. Way too wasted to shower tonight. He got into his bed, stared at the ceiling for a minute, figuring there was no way he was going to fall asleep tonight. All the booze in his bloodstream would keep him up. He passed out moments later. So much for that.

Andy was in deep sleep when the motel front door came crashing in and a swarm of local cops with their guns drawn dragged him out of bed.

Chapter Four

It took Andy a moment to figure out what was going on. These were cops. They had him face down on the floor of his motel room with a knee to the back of his neck, and someone holding down his legs so he couldn't kick out. He didn't even think of kicking out; he was too stunned.

They wrenched his arms behind his back and slapped on a set of handcuffs. He felt the cold steel cut into his wrist bones. He hadn't been arrested in years and vowed never to go through it again. He had done well staying on the right side of the law until now.

One of the cops radioed dispatch, "Yeah. We got the scumbag. Bringing him in now."

Andy racked his brains. What is going on? I just walked straight home, right? He hadn't done anything dumb. They must have the wrong guy. No sense arguing with these thugs. Sit tight. Say nothing and worry about it at the cop station.

His head hurt, and his mouth was drier than the Sahara Desert. He needed water, or Pedialyte, or something.

They hoisted Andy to his feet and grabbed him by the handcuffs.

"Come on, asshole. Time to go," one of the cops snarled at Andy.

Andy was only dressed in his boxers and a t-shirt. They left his jeans, boots, and leather jacket back in his hotel room.

When they dragged him onto the balcony, he was stunned to see multiple cop cars and crime scene units in the motel forecourt. What the hell happened last night?

The two cops rushed Andy downstairs and shoved him into the back of a police cruiser.

"We got him," one of them proudly announced to some of the other cops.

"Watch your head, asshole," the other cop said to Andy, roughly shoving him into the back of the cruiser and shutting the door on him.

The two cops who had dragged him downstairs chatted for a couple of minutes with their colleagues before jumping into their cruiser.

"You fucking asshole," said the smaller of the two cops. "You come to our town and try to pull this shit. Wait till the Sheriff gets a hold of you."

The other chuckled loudly at this.

Still trying to shake off the fog of sleep, Andy wondered what exactly he was meant to have done.

It didn't take long to get to the police station. It was all the way across town on the east side, but being a small town and just past dawn, traffic was light.

The driver took their vehicle around the back of the station, parked up, and jumped out. Seconds later, they pulled open the back door and dragged Andy out.

"Come on, asshole. Move it," said the smaller cop. Andy was really beginning to dislike this little creep.

The bigger cop punched in a code on the back door of the sheriff's station, and they dragged Andy in. They led him down a pristine corridor and into a holding cell. The smaller cop undid the cuffs and shoved Andy in, locking the cell door behind him.

"Hey, can I get a water or something?" Andy begged.

The cop looked at Andy for a moment like he was insane, then simply said, "No," before storming off out of sight.

Fuck that guy, thought Andy.

The one thing with small-town holding cells is that they were barely crowded. In a big city, there would probably be 20–30 guys sitting in there with Andy. He found himself alone. His head hurt, and he was still tired, so he spread out over the bed and tried to nap.

It must have worked, as he soon fell back to sleep. He was rudely awakened some time later by a cop he had never seen before.

"Get up, Harlan, and come with me," instructed the guard.

Andy still felt like dog shit, but at least he wasn't so tired now. He followed the guard, somewhat amused. He hadn't even been charged with anything yet.

"Get in here," said the guard, opening the door to a room.

The first thing Andy noticed was the one-way glass on the opposite side of the room. A lineup? Certainly seemed that way. Moments later, his suspicions were proven true as five other guys shuffled in. What a ridiculous situation. All these men were wearing long pants, and here was he in his boxers and t-shirt. He almost wanted to laugh. What a joke. Besides, at least two of his "peers" were clearly cops. They had that cop look about them. It was quite obvious these were the only men they could rustle up first thing in the morning.

A voice came over the P.A. system.

"Everyone, line up and face the window."

They did so.

"Face right."

They did so.

"Prisoner Two, step forward." The man second closest to the wall stepped up.

"Turn to your right. Okay, thanks. Step back," said the voice.

The man stepped back.

"You. You are in the boxer shorts. Step forward," said the voice.

This is ridiculous, scoffed Andy. How is this fair? I am the only one here in my boxers. What a joke. Regardless, he stepped forward.

"Turn right."

He turned to his right.

"Turn to your left." He turned left.

"Okay, thanks, everyone," said the voice.

WTF, they didn't even ask me to step back in line, thought Andy. That ain't right.

The door opened, and the cop, or guard, or whoever he was, stood there waiting for Andy to shuffle out. The rest of the men nodded or greeted Andy's new buddy as they exited the room. So they all know each other, thought Andy.

"This way," said Andy's escort.

The cop led Andy into another room. He knew what type of room this was: an "interview" room. Andy knew the drill from his wild and reckless early 20s. Give your name and address and say nothing more. Insist on a lawyer. Sign nothing, no matter what tough talk or threats they throw at you. He was mentally prepared.

"Can I get you anything?" asked the cop.

"Uh, yeah," said Andy. "A bottle of water. Oh, and what about a pair of pants?"

"Sure thing. What size pants do you wear? 36"? 38"?" asked the cop.

"34," Thanks," said Andy.

"What about shoes?" asked the guard.

"Shoes? Oh yeah, that would be nice. Size 11. Thanks."

The cop left. Andy could hear him locking the door on the way out. What did they think Andy was going to do? Try to make a run for it? Some fool probably would try.

Two minutes later, the cop turned up with a bottle of water and a pair of prison scrubs.

"Here ya go," said the cop, leaving both on the table and exiting. Once again, Andy could hear him lock the door behind him.

Andy grabbed the pants and checked them out. The tag said "Medium." Hopefully, they would fit. To his surprise, they fit well.

He checked out the sneakers the guard left him. They were like Vans slip-ons, but a cheap knockoff version. Typical government agency, buying the cheapest crap, thought Andy, slipping on the flimsy shoes.

Andy eyed up the jacket. It wasn't cold, so he looked at it and slung it over the back of his chair.

He cracked open the bottle of water and chugged half of it down. His mouth was so damn dry; the cold water was a welcome relief.

Andy sat and waited. He knew their game. Make you wait. And wait. And wait. Then the nice, concerned detective comes in, asks you some seemingly harmless questions, and tries to get you to incriminate yourself. You don't fall for it. Well, he makes his excuses and leaves. Then the bad-ass detective comes in and goes all tough guy on you. Threats, shouting, and possibly physical intimidation. Probably been going on since the dawn of law enforcement: good cop, bad cop. He still had no clue why he had been dragged out of bed. He assumed something last night. Maybe someone's car got scratched up? Maybe some local kid threw a brick through a store owner's store windows? Andy figured they would soon come in and lay their cards on the table.

He planned to tell them his name and address, and that was it. Then he would insist on a lawyer. He didn't know any lawyers here in town, and he certainly didn't have the money to pay for a lawyer, but he would insist on one. Wasn't that the American way? You had a right to a lawyer, and if you couldn't afford one, you would be assigned one. Of course, the lawyer would be at the bottom of the barrel, but any lawyer was better than trying to defend yourself.

More time passed. Andy didn't have a watch on, but he guessed a good 30 minutes had gone by. Wow, they were really playing the "let's keep him waiting" game today.

He reached for his half-drunk bottle of water to have another drink. Just as the bottle reached his lips, one of the sheriff's deputies entered the room. Without saying a word, he walked right up to Andy and punched him in the side of the head.

Andy dropped his bottle of water and yelped, "Ouch! What the fuck?"

The cop hit him again.

Oh, I get it, thought Andy. These guys want to slap me around, and the moment I hit back, I get arrested for assaulting a police officer. Nice try, douchebags.

"You murdering piece of shit," snarled the cop as he swung on Andy again. This shot to his temple rocked Andy so much that he fell off his chair. The cop turned and walked out.

Andy got to his feet and back onto his chair. His head was still pounding. Oh, I get it, he thought. They are doing "bad cop" first, then good cop. He was on to them. That said, did he say murder? What?

Another sheriff's deputy walked in.

"Okay, Mr. Harlan, we would like you to tell us your version of events," said the Sheriff.

"What events?" asked Andy.

"Of last night," the Sheriff replied.

"I went and had a couple of drinks and went back to my motel and straight to bed," answered Andy.

"After you killed David Nichols?" asked the Sheriff.

"What? Wait, who is David Nichols?" asked Andy.

What was it? A drug deal gone bad? Guns?" asked the Sheriff.

"Sheriff, I have no idea who this David Nichols is," said Andy.

"So you never saw the guy in the room next to yours?" asked the Sheriff. "We have an eyewitness who places you at the scene of the crime!"

Andy was starting to get pissed off now. Was this some weird small-town intimidation tactic to get "undesirables" out of town, or was this guy thinking he was serious?

"What are you talking about?" snapped Andy. This wasn't good; he was losing his temper. Losing his cool now would make him fall right into their hands.

"You met up with Mr. Nichols in his motel room. You ripped him off. Things went badly. You killed him and thought you could get away with it."

"Look, Sheriff. I already told you I have ZERO involvement in whatever it is you are accusing me of. I want a lawyer."

"No one who is innocent needs a lawyer," sneered the Sheriff.

"Lawyer," Andy repeated.

"Very well. Be that way. Just be aware a lawyer is going to take a few hours to track down," said the Sheriff.

It was probably true, but Andy knew from experience that a lot of cops would tell you that, and an unsuspecting sap might think they could still talk their way out of any charges before their lawyer arrives and usually dig themselves into an even deeper mess by doing so. He was determined to keep quiet until a lawyer arrived.

"Lawyer," Andy repeated again.

"Very well. Be that way," said the deputy before getting up and exiting the interview room.

Andy's head hurt. Being hungover and then being hit repeatedly in the side of the head would do that to a person.

The door opened again. Two more sheriff's deputies entered.

"Okay, scumbag, come with us," said the older of the two deputies.

Andy got up, figuring they would take him back to the holding cells. Instead, they went the other way.

To his bewilderment, Andy was fingerprinted, photographed, and charged with murder. What a joke. No forensic evidence, nothing. Just the say-so from some supposed eyewitness. Who was that? The motel clerk? The woman he passed on the staircase coming back last night? Either way, they had nothing on him. He was innocent, and even an inexperienced law school graduate could get this case thrown out in five minutes. Andy wasn't stressing just yet. Plus, he had been assaulted; it might be a nice payday in a personal damages lawsuit once he got out of this mess.

The two law enforcement officers then escorted Andy back to his cell. After they locked him back up, one of them returned with a juice box and a sandwich. What was he, five years old?

Regardless, he ate the sandwich. At least some food in his stomach might mop up the booze in his system. He hadn't drunk a juice box in at least 30 years, but he was grateful for the hydration.

He was just finishing his juice box when the big cop who had roughed him up in the interrogation room arrived at Andy's cell. He opened the door, walked up to Andy, and cracked him again in the side of the head. That was it. Already charged with murder, Andy was in no mood for this goon. He jumped up and started fighting back. He got a couple of good body shots to the bigger man's ribs and was setting up for a head shot when two more sheriff's deputies rushed his cell. One of them cracked him in the back of his head, and he felt his legs buckle from under him as he went down for the count. The last thing he remembered was getting kicked in the back.

Chapter Five

Andy woke up on the floor of his cell. He wasn't sure if his nose was broken, but he couldn't breathe through it, and it was coagulated with blood. He could taste blood in his mouth, too. His whole body hurt. Rotten bastards kicking a man when he was down and passed out. No honor, no nothing.

It hurt to move. He cleared his nostrils, but even the effort of getting his right hand to his face hurt. He lay there on the floor, pondering whether it was worth even attempting the effort to sit up. As he lay there contemplating his next move, he could hear two of what he assumed were law enforcement talking up the hallway.

"What do you mean?" the first voice said.

"I told you. They caught the guy who did it. That guy is innocent," said the second voice.

"No way. Look at him. He was definitely involved. Even the eyewitness could place him at the scene," said the first voice.

"No, no. She said she saw him on the stairwell. That was it. He could have just been going to his room," said the second voice.

"Dude, you sure on this?" asked the first voice.

"Yeah, totally sure. Caught the dude in Sedona," said the second voice.

"Well, fuck," said the first voice.

"I know! I know. That's what I have been trying to tell you!" said the second voice.

"So, what do we do with him?" asked the first voice.

"I dunno, man. Sheriff Brantley will decide," said the second voice.

"Oh shit. You mean…?" said the first voice.

"Yes. He loves that option. You know…" said the second voice.

Andy struggled to hear more of the conversation, but it got fainter as they walked further from his cell. He knew right away they were talking about him. Finally, some justice! Only a matter of time now, and these bullshit charges would be dropped, and he would be set free. Fucking assholes. He would definitely be visiting one of those "ambulance chaser" lawyers when he got back to Phoenix. No, doctor's office first. Get all his injuries factually documented immediately, and then send them to the lawyer's office. One of those guys who advertises on billboards and the sides of Phoenix Metro buses. Those guys would be like pit bulls fighting for his case. These creeps were going to be very, very sorry they ever crossed paths with Andy Harlan when he got out. He would make them pay. All of them.

Andy passed out again.

Chapter Six

Andy woke up to feel a knee pressing hard into his back, right between his shoulder blades. It hurt like hell. Someone grabbed his right arm and wrenched it behind his back. Then his left arm. He felt the cold steel of the handcuffs cutting into his wrists as they cuffed him up. He was in a lot of pain, but was determined not to let these cops know how hurt he was. All he could assume was that if he was getting cuffed, they must be ready to let him go. Fine. They would be getting their own portion of pain when they all lost their jobs and were paying out for what they had done to him.

He was roughly pulled to his feet, and then someone shoved a black hood over his head. He could see light or dark from the overhead lights, but that was all he could see. He figured they didn't want him being able to describe their faces in a court of law once they let him go. So be it. Andy was confident he could pick out at least three of these fuckers, especially the big ox who attacked him in both the interrogation room and his jail cell.

Andy was escorted down the hall, away from the main part of the police station. He felt the blast of warm air as they exited the building. The car park! They were taking him out of the building. This was probably good. Dropped off at the hotel, probably told to leave town and not come back. Don't worry, assholes, I'll be back and with hot-shot lawyers to sue you into the next century. Pricks.

He heard them pop the back doors of some form of van. One of the two deputies got in before him, and between the two cops, they hoisted him into the van and onto a bench seat. He could feel them sitting on either side of him. Then he heard a voice.

"Ready?" asked one of his escorts.

"Just waiting on the others," another voice replied, clearly sitting in the front of the van.

So there were three of them in this van, and they were waiting for others? How many guys do they need to take one biker back to his motel?

A few moments later, Andy heard other voices in the car park talking to the driver of his van. It seemed like they were laughing and joking. That was a good thing, right? Light-heartedness meant they were letting him go. He could deal with that. Take me back to my motel. Get these cuffs off me and let me leave town. Thanks for nothing. He would be back and seek vengeance on them, but for now, he would bide his time.

Finally, he heard another vehicle in the car park start up. Then the van he was in started up. It was happening. They were on the move. Not long now, he would be on his Harley and heading out of town.

Andy tried to keep up with the turns they were making. Right out of the car park, a left here, a right there. So far, so good. The van kept moving. The cops in his van were silent. No small talk. No jokes. No sports talk. Was that normal? He wasn't sure.

They were still traveling. Andy found that when he was thinking about the cops in his van, he had forgotten to keep track of the turns they were making. All of a sudden, it dawned on him that they were heading the wrong way.

Chapter Seven

This wasn't good. They were heading in the wrong direction. For what purpose? To drop him on the outskirts of town in his prison scrubs and flimsy sneakers?

Andy tried to keep a mental count of how long they were driving for. At first, he was doing the one, one thousand, two, one thousand count, but soon got distracted. He tried to just guesstimate after that, but for all he knew, his count was going to be way off. Regardless of how time he assumed this was all taking, he had enough sense to realize it was way longer than it should have been to get even to Sedona. Something was amiss.

It seemed to Andy that they had now taken a turn off the main road and onto a dirt road. They must be heading south and west again, as if they were purely heading east, they would have passed by Sedona or another well-populated town. What the heck were they thinking?

Another left turn. It seemed they were climbing now. Up a hill perhaps? A few bumps as well. What were they playing at?

Finally, after what Andy guessed was a good forty-five minutes after leaving the police station, they came to a stop. He heard the driver shut the van down. Okay, something was about to go down. After the day he had had so far, he assumed nothing good.

Andy heard the van driver exit their vehicle. He could hear him talking to someone, but not what they were saying. So there was at least one more group of guys here. Had they followed Andy's vehicle, or was this other group already here and waiting?

After a bit more conversation, Andy's driver re-entered the van.

"He says we have to hold off for a few," said the driver. "Big storm blowing through. As soon as it's over, well..."

"Got it," said the cop sitting on Andy's left.

"Yeah, looks like it's going to be a heavy one," said the other cop sitting in back with Andy.

Andy was used to these types of storms. It was the end of the monsoon season. Summers in Arizona were very, very hot, and it barely rained in the winters, but at the end of summer, sometimes you would get a month's worth of rain dumped on you in a day. If it weren't raining, you could also expect sandstorms (which the locals called Haboobs), which were often even more deadly.

Outside the van, Andy could hear the wind picking up. In the old days, as kids, when they heard that noise, it was a sign to race home or seek out cover. Then came the first drops of rain on the windows of the van. Despite having a hood on, Andy could still make out light and dark, but the light was getting less and less. Definitely a big storm coming in. Then he heard the thunder and lightning. It sounded close.

The spitting rain soon became a torrential downpour, slapping the side of the van hard. It must be a crazy one, as even the cops locked in with Andy were making comments about it. Andy sat and listened. When in doubt, it's best to stay silent and try to formulate some form of plan. Maybe he could make a break for it in the middle of the storm. If one of the guys in the back opened those rear doors, he could flick off the hood, attack the remaining guard, and make a run for it? Feeble plan, but that's all he could think of to do.

Time passed. He heard the van driver tell one of the sheriff's deputies in the back that it was just after one pm.

Andy was thirsty; he contemplated asking them for water. He was a great believer in the age-old saying, "If you don't ask, you don't get." What's the worst that could happen? They say no? Well, actually, the worst that could happen had already happened. They had beaten him senseless. Fuck these guys. Maybe by making demands on them, they would get taken off guard. It was worth a try. Besides, he was actually thirsty.

"Hey, fellas, any chance of a refreshing beverage?" Andy asked.

He had surprised them. It's almost like they had forgotten he was with them, or that he was awake, or something. Perhaps by being quiet for so long, they had assumed he had passed out or was asleep.

"No," said the driver.

"Oh, come on, man. Even a prisoner of war has some basic rights," Andy countered. Now he was just doing it to mess with them.

"He's right, Max," said the cop on Andy's left. "Pass me that water bottle, would ya?"

Andy could feel the other cop reaching over him. He heard the familiar noise of a bottle cap being twisted off.

"Now if I give you this water, no funny business, alright?" said the cop on Andy's left.

"No. No funny business, man. I'm just super thirsty," said Andy.

The cop lifted Andy's hood just enough to reveal his mouth. The cop then held the water bottle to Andy's mouth.

"Here ya go, asshole," said the cop.

Andy chugged the water. He was genuinely thirsty. He needed to drink. But at the same time, by lifting the hood even partially, Andy could see it was almost pitch black and stormy outside the safety and comfort of the van. Ahh, got to love monsoon season.

"Thanks," said Andy after drinking half the bottle. The cop pulled the hood back down and put the bottle away somewhere in the van.

The storm raged overhead; winds and rain battered their police van. Just as Andy was beginning to think it would never end, he could hear it slowing down.

Okay, so whatever these assholes have got planned for me, I guess I will soon find out, thought Andy to himself.

Sure enough, the rain slowed down, and the wind had passed over them.

Max, the van driver, got out of the van again. Andy strained to hear what was going on outside. Definitely some voices talking, but try as he might, he couldn't pick out any words. Nothing that might give him a clue what they were fixing for him.

Andy heard footfalls approaching the van. Then the back doors were yanked open.

"Okay, bring him out," said the voice. It was definitely not Max's voice.

The two cops who had been sitting on either side of Andy grabbed him and led him out of the van, keeping his hood in place.

"Get him on his knees," commanded the voice.

Andy braced himself for the worst. They were going to kill him out here and dump his body. Those fuckers. Well, if ya kill me now, I will come back and haunt you fuckers for the rest of your wretched lives, thought Andy.

"All right. Remove his hood," said the voice.

They ripped his hood off. Andy scrunched his eyes up as he adjusted to daylight. Looking up, he was faced by an older sheriff with a pistol on his hip and two deputies pointing shotguns at him. This was it.

"Afternoon, asshole. I'm Sheriff Eli Brantley, Eli to my friends, but you can call me sir," said Sheriff Eli Brantley.

Andy chose to say nothing.

"You're in deep shit, son, coming to our town and causing trouble. We don't stand for that in Blackwood Ridge," Sheriff Eli continued.

"You tell him, uncle," sniggered one of the cops holding a shotgun on Andy.

"I will tell you what, though," said Sheriff Eli. "I'm a reasonable man. I believe in second chances."

Yeah, right, thought Andy.

"Here's what I am prepared to do," said Sheriff Eli. "I'm prepared to give you a sporting chance."

"Okay," said Andy.

"I'll give you a dirt bike and a one-hour head start. If you make it out of Blackwood Ridge, then we will let you go. A free man. On my word."

Sheriff Eli's nephew grinned and nodded his head.

"And what if I don't want to play your sick game?" asked Andy.

Eli looked at his five deputies. "Well, then we can just shoot ya right here."

Eli's nephew sniggered again. It was only then that Andy spotted the big deputy who had beaten the snot out of him, wheeling a dirt bike towards the Sheriff. He hated that guy with a vengeance.

Andy contemplated his options. At least if he got out of here, he could do something to shut these fuckers down. Bring them to justice.

"So which way is the border of Blackwood Ridge County?" asked Andy.

"Oh no. Where's the fun in that?" smiled Sheriff Eli.

"Okay. I'll take the deal. How do I know you will keep your side of the deal, though?" Andy asked.

"This is Blackwood Ridge County, son. We always honor our deals," said Sheriff Eli.

"Okay, so I have your word," said Andy.

"Yes, sir," said Sheriff Eli's nephew.

"Hey Tommy, you gas up that dirt bike?" asked Sheriff Eli to the big cop.

"Yes, Sheriff, I did," said Tommy.

"Okay, son, you have one hour. Good luck to you," said Sheriff Eli. "Uncuff him, boys."

One of Andy's escorts undid his cuffs. He rubbed his wrists; he noticed the skin was raw and inflamed on his right wrist. Those assholes.

Andy stood up and stretched his legs. From the beating he took to sitting on the bench seats of the cop van for God knows how many hours, he was stiff and sore. Every muscle ached. That said, he was determined to make it out of Blackwood Ridge alive and bring these assholes to justice.

"Well, come on, son, we ain't got all day," smiled Sheriff Eli.

Andy walked over to the piece-of-shit dirt bike and looked it over. Seems like it had been lying in the back of a barn for the last forty years.

"Does it even run?" he asked Big Tommy.

"Yeah, I had it running this morning," grinned Tommy.

Andy fired up the old dirt bike and let the engine idle for a moment. Despite being close to forty years old, it actually did run. These Japanese bikes were pretty much indestructible, thought Andy.

"Start the clock," said Sheriff Eli to one of the deputies. "You got fifty-nine minutes left, dipshit."

Andy looked back at the Sheriff and the deputies. One way or another, he was going to bring these guys down.

Andy straddled the old dirt bike and gave the throttle a little twist. Okay, it still had some guts left in her. He released the clutch and pulled out, heading back down the dirt road he assumed they had arrived on.

Behind him, he could hear a couple of the deputies hooting and hollering.

Chapter Eight

Andy cruised back down the dirt road. Once he got out of sight of the cops, he realized he needed a strategy. If he continued down the road, they could probably catch him with ease. Besides, who's to say they would give him a full hour to make his getaway? They would probably get antsy after thirty minutes and give chase. He needed to think of a plan.

About half a mile down the dirt road and to his right, Andy spotted a small forest of pine trees. One advantage two wheels had over four was that he could get his bike into places that their vehicles could not go. That was it. He would cut across and through the forest to lose these assholes.

Andy paused for a moment to look back before turning off the dirt road and into the forest. No sign of his tormentors following him. Good. How long had it been so far? Ten minutes? Fifteen?

He lifted himself slightly off the seat so his legs could absorb the bumps and berms of the ground before the forest. Once into the forest, he dodged and weaved his way through the ancient trees, trying not to lose any speed as he did so. Ain't no way these fools were going to be able to follow him in their vehicles. They would have to get out and walk after him to give chase, and even then, he had the advantage of the old bike to get him ahead of these guys. Had they miscalculated? Or was Andy overoptimistic?

After a couple of miles, he came to a clearing, open ground ahead. No sign of a road. That was good. He highly doubted that they would be able to catch him now. Once again, he lifted his butt off the seat so his legs could absorb the impact of all the bumps as he rode across the rough ground. He rode up and down a series of small hills and valleys, making good distance between himself and the forest behind him. Maybe, just maybe, he had a chance here.

He continued on, heading west. He climbed another small hill, and to his horror, he saw he was faced with a sheer cliff drop ahead. No way around it. He had to turn back. Dammit. Now where?

Andy swung the dirt bike around and rode up the next hill and back down again, retracing his steps. He just climbed to the top of the next small incline when, to his horror, he saw one of the cop SUVs heading right for him. Dammit! How? There was no way. Unless, what if they had some sort of tracking device hidden on his dirt bike? He hadn't even thought to check it. Maybe one of those AirPods? There was no other way to explain how this guy had found Andy so fast. He turned the bike around. He had no choice but to head back the way he had come. The cop's SUV was gaining fast on Andy. Damn four-wheel drives! In a battle between an SUV and a bike, four wheels were always going to win. The law of gross tonnage had never been beaten.

The solo cop driving the SUV was gaining on Andy fast. He had no doubt this bastard was trying to run him down. Maybe, just maybe, he could lure the cop to the cliff edge and turn away at the last second. Bad plan, but that was all he had. He could literally feel the SUV behind him now. He twisted the throttle and made a little prayer that he wouldn't run out of gas right now. One more hill to climb, one more valley to descend, and then the cliff drop. This asshole was gaining.

He could see the cliff edge ahead of him. The SUV wasn't slowing down. That told Andy that the cop was hyper-focused on running him down and not looking ahead. Andy waited till the very last moment, then twisted his handlebars to veer out of the way. He turned too suddenly and low-sided. All he knew now was he had to roll out of the way to avoid being crushed by the cop's wheels.

It was at that moment that he heard the cop trying to slam on the brakes and avoid the cliff's edge. It was too late. He was going so fast, and his tires couldn't grip the dirt fast enough. Andy's bike went over the edge, the cop and his SUV went over the edge, and Andy slid across the dirt toward the cliff's edge a little to the right. He grabbed clumps of dirt with his bare hands as he tried to slow himself down. Below, he could hear the cop's SUV crashing and thumping on whatever rocks waited below. In a moment, he would be joining them at the bottom of the ravine.

Andy managed to roll from his back to his belly as he slid closer and closer to the edge. He managed to grab a clump of dirt with his right hand, but it tore away, only slowing him momentarily. He felt his legs go over the edge; he braced himself for the deadly impact that waited for him below.

Chapter Nine

Just for a moment, Andy's bruised and battered body was airborne. He then hit the dirt slope with an undignified thump. The spot he had gone over the edge was nowhere near as steep as where the cop and the dirt bike had gone over, which had been a sheer drop. That said, Andy was sliding down the side of the cliff face. His butt and back were getting busted up with each bump that he hit. At least he was still alive. He scrambled to grab a tree root, a branch, anything to slow his fall. Finally, after a good thirty feet of slipping and sliding, he managed to cling to a rock. He had stopped his descent.

Andy took a moment to get his breath back. His heart was pounding, and adrenaline coursed through his body. He had no bike, and he was halfway down the ravine. Surely the cop who had been pursuing him had radioed it in. If not, perhaps the cop had a tracking device in his vehicle alerting the others to his location. If Andy did manage to climb back up, surely he would run into the others in time. With no dirt bike, he would be on foot. He would be a goner for sure. He had no choice but to continue to descend into the bottom of the canyon. Maybe then he could find a way out.

Finally, after a ton of effort on his bruised and battered body, he made it to the bottom of the canyon. There was a riverbed, but it was pretty dry. Just a few puddles of dirty water. At least if the water was flowing, he could risk straining it through his t-shirt and attempt to drink some. No luck. With no real idea where he was, Andy decided to continue heading west since the cops had come in from the east. He traversed the dry riverbed looking for anything he could scavenge.

In his teenage years, he and his friends would explore and camp in these canyons, but they always had some tools at least: a buck knife, a compass, a water bottle, a water filter, and tents. Andy had nothing but the will to survive. He was okay for now, but he would need water before too long. He continued trudging west.

The sun was starting to get low in the sky. Before long, he would have to seek some form of shelter. Walking in the dark might save him from detection by the pursuing cops, but could also be dangerous when you can't see where you are going: twist an ankle, fall into a hole, or worse still, walk right off a cliff. Besides, he was so exhausted that he needed to rest.

Ahead, something orange-colored flapping in the wind caught his eye. It was one of those disposable rain ponchos that tourists would wear to Niagara Falls or something. He walked over to see if anything else had been discarded nearby. Nothing. Regardless, he grabbed the poncho and wadded it up. Might come in handy later. Andy continued west. After another bend in the river, the canyon came to a fork. Both options would take him further west; however, one would be southwest and the other northwest. On a whim, he chose northwest. He trudged on. The prison-issue sneakers were hurting his feet. He would definitely need to stop soon. He listened carefully and could hear no signs of his pursuers.

Andy walked for another twenty minutes or so. He needed to find shelter and fast. On the canyon floor, the sun was already dipping below the horizon. He looked around to see if there was any possible place to hide out for the night. Then he saw it, up on high: ancient cave dwellings from the Native American Puebloans.

They always reminded Andy of some form of old high-rise apartment buildings. Some were only accessible with handmade wooden ladders, which he didn't have, and some had handholds cut into the rocks. Maybe he would get lucky.

He headed toward the cliff dwellings. After a bit of searching, he found a way to climb toward them. Nearly slipping a few times, he made it to the first structure. It looked like a food or grain storage place. The residences would be further along the cliff face. Food storage first, main housing second. As he slowly made his way across the small pathway, he risked a look down. Had to be a good seventy-five to one hundred feet drop. He was glad he was not trying to traverse this in pitch-black darkness. One wrong step and over you go. Splat.

He entered the main house. No one had been here for a very long time. When were these built? Five hundred years ago? Seven hundred? To build up here would have been risky, even dangerous. To build up here, you had to have a reason. Who were the people here protecting themselves from? Warring tribes? Enemy invaders? Andy figured he would never know.

He explored the main room, now in semi-darkness. Was there anything beyond this structure? He exited the building and decided to go investigate. Sure enough, one more building along the cliff face. It was only then that he noticed a gap of about seven to eight feet with no pathway. Straight drop to the rocks below. This must have been the people's "safe" room. Some of these cliff dwellers would have a wooden ladder to scale vertically, but also another wooden ladder to scale horizontally. He looked around. There it was, tucked into a corner. An ancient log. Would it hold his weight? He grabbed it and exerted some pressure on it. Still seemed sturdy, but he wouldn't trust it more than once or twice.

He grabbed it and laid it down across the treacherous gap. Even then, he tested to make sure it would not slip out of place the moment he stepped onto it.

Andy was hungry. There was no chance of grabbing any food anytime soon. Even if he caught a rabbit or some small animal, he would need to skin it and cook it. He would be all right for a day or two. Water was a different story. He would need some in the morning. The air was still damp; perhaps he could use the rain poncho to collect some dew overnight? There was no place near the "safe" room to hang it. There was space behind him before the main cliff residence. He returned to the area and spotted a good place to hang up the poncho. He grabbed some small rocks to keep it in place. Satisfied it would stay in place, he returned to the main house. It was getting dark now. He needed to cross the gap to the "safe" room before he couldn't see what he was doing. Andy tested the ladder/bridge one more time before crossing the gap. Relieved he had made it without the ladder cracking under his weight, he pulled it up and brought it into the safe room. That way, he could rest in peace without having to fear waking up to a shotgun aimed at him.

He managed to find a corner to get comfortable in and curled up in an attempt to get some rest. Within minutes, he had fallen into a deep sleep.

Andy woke the next day, confused about where he was. It took him a minute to realize he was in that safe room of the cliff dwelling and what had happened to him. Moving his body was a grim reminder of the two beatings, plus the slide off the dirt bike had done to his poor, abused body. Everything hurt. He was hungry too, but had resigned himself to not eating until he made it out of this mess. He was thirsty as hell, though. It felt like he had spent a night drinking with the Phoenix Motorcycle Club, the Steel Reapers. He needed hydration. It was at that moment that he remembered hanging up the rain poncho from the night before.

He stood up and tried to stretch a bit to loosen up his battered body. He grabbed the wooden ladder, put it in place across the seven-foot gap, and made sure it was secure. He then quickly scaled the divide, making sure he didn't look down. He passed the main dwelling and went to check on his makeshift tarp. It had worked! He had actually collected some moisture. All in all, he had probably accumulated a little over a cup's worth of water. He put his mouth near the edge of the tarp and maneuvered the water towards him. There was a little bit of dirt and dust, but at that moment, he didn't care. He drank it down greedily, momentarily refreshed. He was pondering his next move when he heard the noise, the all-too-familiar squawk of a police radio. Shit, it was close by. One of the cops must have spotted the orange rain poncho and was climbing up to investigate.

Andy grabbed his tarp and made his way back past the main residence. He probably only had moments to cross the gap to the safe room and remove the wooden ladder. He crossed the gap in a split second and removed the ladder, taking it into the safe room. It was then that he heard a voice, one of the cops. He couldn't make out all of the conversation, but he did hear the word "investigate." What could he do? He couldn't fight the guy. Fists against a gun? He wasn't Superman. He decided the best he could do was stay hidden and hope the cop didn't come and check out the safe room.

He could hear the guy thumping about in one of the other buildings, but Andy couldn't be sure if it was the food larder or the main residence. Sound bounced off the walls here, making it hard to gauge. He stayed still, trying to slow his breathing and his heart rate. Then, to his horror, he heard the cop cursing. He must have spied the gap between the main dwelling and the safe room.

Don't try it. Don't try it. Don't try it, he said to himself. If he fought the guy, chances are the others would be on him in minutes.

Then he heard the one noise he didn't want to hear, the cop running and jumping over the gap. With a sickening thud, he heard the impact of the man's body as he slammed into this side of the precipice. Just as he was bracing himself to fight the guy, he heard a "Ahh shit, no!" then "Fuck fuck help help." The guy was still there. Had he slipped on the edge or broken his ankle?

Andy's brain quickly ran through his options. Kick the guy and send him spiraling to his doom? Help him up? No way. He could not trust any of these crooked cops. What if he saved the guy's life and then the guy just shot him? He was torn. He was not a stone-cold killer, but at the same time, if he helped the guy, he was signing his own death warrant. He didn't know what to do.

Chapter Ten

At the last moment, Andy decided, regardless of what these cops had put him through, he was going to have to risk it and save the guy. Let fate take its course. He exited the safe room and made his way to the gap. It was the big cop who had beaten him senseless in the police station. The cop was hanging onto the edge of the cliff by his arms, and most of his body was dangling precariously below. When he saw Andy appear, his eyes went wide with fear.

"Here!" said Andy, extending his hand. As the big cop went to reach for Andy's hand, the edge of the gap gave way, sending the man to his death. Their eyes locked for a split second before the cop cascaded to his doom. That one-second look would stay with Andy for the rest of his life.

The big guy screamed for a second, then there was a dull thump that Andy heard from one hundred feet above. If the man wasn't dead now, he would be in minutes. No human body was made to withstand a fall like that.

He had sworn vengeance on the guy, but not like that. Still, part of him was glad that he had at least tried to save the guy.

It was time to leave. No doubt his buddies would come looking for Andy soon enough and blame him for their buddy's death. They were going to be more pissed off now. Who would believe him? No one. He had to move. He descended back down to the riverbed below.

Andy continued heading west into the canyon. He had gone a couple of miles when he heard someone shout a blood-curdling "NOOO."

It was a male voice. He could only assume that the rest of the cops hunting him down had discovered the body of their colleague. The next thing he knew, he heard multiple semi-automatic pistols firing. He instinctively ducked and hit the dirt, but then it dawned on him that they must be firing at the cave dwellings up high. These guys were enraged, incensed even at the loss of their workmate, and were screaming for vengeance. He had to stay ahead of them. God knows what would happen if they caught up to him. Actually, he did know. They would torture him and kill him, probably torture him again after he was dead, too. His only hope was to find a way out of this canyon and get clear away from Blackwood Ridge.

The way westward twisted and turned. On occasion, he could hear the voices of the men hunting him. The sound bounced over the canyon walls, making it very hard to tell how close or how far away they were from him. He didn't have the energy to break into a full-paced run, so he would run a few steps, walk to get his breath back, and run a few steps. Anything to keep out of range of whatever weapons they were carrying.

Andy got to another bend in the canyon, leading him slightly more north but still west as well. He could no longer hear the cops pursuing him, and his feet were killing him, so he slipped off his prison-issue sneakers and socks for a moment. He flexed his feet and wriggled his toes to try to give them a break. Spying a small pool of water in the dried-up riverbed, he walked over and soaked his feet for a moment. He had to admit, it felt great.

He resigned himself to moving on again when he felt an old and familiar rumbling. What was that? An earthquake? Nah. Never got earthquakes in this part of Arizona. He knew what it was, but his brain was so scrambled, he couldn't think. Then he saw some rabbits running toward him at a high rate of speed.

Of course! It was a flash flood. This was the season for them. It had been so long that he had forgotten. Back in junior high school, three boys from his class had been exploring the canyons near town when a flash flood had occurred. All three were washed away. They found the bodies of two of the boys, but the third body was never found. It had shocked the town for a long time.

Andy raced back to his sneakers and socks and, without hesitating to put them on, scrambled to higher ground. It was actually slightly easier to climb barefoot, something the Native Americans had figured out thousands of years ago.

He had clambered up on a rock a good twenty feet off the ground when he saw the first rush of flood waters come flying by. It really was a flash flood. Not only did you run the risk of drowning, getting caught up in the flood waters, but you also ran the risk of getting crushed against rocks and trees. Not a good scene.

The flow of water built up in speed and size. Andy sat safely above, relieved that he had figured out in time to get the hell out of the way. There was no surviving the onslaught. It was loud too. So very loud. He thought somewhere in the distance, he heard a man screaming. Had one of the cops been caught up in the floodwaters?

He didn't plan to stick around to find out. From his position perched above the flood waters, he spied a small, worn-in path leading to the top of the cliff. Goats? Mountain lions? Regardless of which animals had created the path, he was grateful. He pulled on his socks, slipped on his shoes, and clambered up the path that would lead him to the top.

After a few near slips and some skinned knuckles, Andy made it out of the canyon. But where was he? He had no clue. He could no longer hear the rushing water below, but wasn't sure if he wanted to keep heading west. Maybe North would be a better option now? He decided to walk a little to the east and see what he could see, then return to where he was and maybe head north. If nothing showed promise in either of those directions, he would carry on west.

Andy walked back half a mile to the east. There seemed to be nothing in the way of civilization in that direction. He was close to the edge of the cliff, and curiosity got the best of him. He inched to the very edge and peered over. Then he could see the riverbed below. The flooding had ended. He was about to assume that law enforcement would now be picking up his trail again when he noticed it: three bodies crushed and tangled together, smashed up against a large jagged rock formation. It was those cops hunting him down. He waited for a moment, but none of them moved. Three dead. Drowned or likely battered to death in the flood waters. How many cops were there now? He ran a quick calculation. That was five. That left one in pursuit of him. But where was he? Continuing west along the riverbed, or currently clambering up the cliff face? He had to get moving again. The last thing he needed was to make it this far and get shot in the back.

He decided to head north. No real reason. He just figured he had already traveled countless miles west, and to follow along the top of the cliff, he had a better chance of running into the final cop. There was a small hill to the north. Perhaps if he climbed that, he would have a better view of the surrounding area.

His feet were really hurting now. Still, they would heal in time. A bullet in his back would not. He soldiered on. It took an estimated thirty minutes to make it to the top of the hill. As he was climbing to the top, he made sure to keep looking back to make sure whoever was following him wouldn't have a clear shot at him. So far, so good. No sign of the missing cop. Maybe he got lucky and the last cop had been washed away, but just to a separate part of the canyon? One could only hope.

Andy reached the top of the hill and decided to get down on his belly to make himself less easy to spot, just in case he was still being tracked by the final cop. From his vantage point, he looked to the north, and to his surprise, he thought he could spy a road in the distance! Salvation! Well, not quite. He would have to make his way there and then wait for a car to come along and make sure it wasn't law enforcement. His mind raced over multiple horror movies where the final survivor thought they were getting away, only to be jumped by the crazed mutants while waiting for a car to pick them up. He would remain cautious.

Inspired by the fact that he had a chance of survival, Andy made it to the road as quickly as possible. He found a decent-sized tree. He decided he would look both ways for vehicles, and if anything even looked remotely close to a cop car, he would disappear into the bushes before they spotted him. Weak plan, but he couldn't think of anything else.

It had to be mid-afternoon now, judging by the position of the sun in the sky. The road he was standing on ran west to east. He had no clue what was nearby and how often cars traveled this route. He made up his mind he would take a ride in either direction. Just let fate carry him along. Besides, who in this day and age hitchhikes? It wasn't the '70s anymore. He would be lucky if anyone stopped for him. Andy was just glad he was wearing a regular T-shirt and not a prison/jail shirt. That, plus the prison-issue pants, would have locals calling law enforcement immediately. He might look disheveled right now, but he definitely didn't look like an escapee.

Finally, he spied a truck heading his way from the west. This was either going to go well or end terribly. His luck had held up so far. He had to have faith he would get through this okay.

As the truck got closer, Andy could see it was not a police vehicle. It was an old, battered Ford truck from the early '80s, possibly the late '70s. A grizzled old farmer was driving. He pulled over.

"What happened to you, son?" he asked, looking Andy over up and down.

"I was hiking in one of the canyons and nearly got caught by a flash flood," Andy lied, thinking on his feet. "Lost all my camping gear and supplies."

The old timer chuckled. "Happens every year around this time. You need a ride, son?"

"Yeah, that would be great. Much appreciated. Where ya headed?" asked Andy, opening the passenger door.

"Just picking up some supplies. A small town about three miles away called Blackwood Ridge. Does that work for you?" asked the old geezer.

"Blackwood Ridge? Yes, that would be perfect. Many thanks. Oh, I'm Andy, by the way," Andy extended his hand for the old farmer to shake.

The old guy shook it. He had a firm grip, obviously from a lifetime of working with his hands. "I'm Gus. Nice to meet ya."

The odd couple made small talk as they made the short trip back to Blackwood Ridge. Andy couldn't believe how close he had gotten to town. The way the cops had driven him out to the drop-off point, he would have assumed they were hundreds of miles away. Perhaps they had been some distance, and traversing the canyons had been a shortcut back to town?

Gus dropped Andy a block from his hotel. He thanked the old man and made the short walk back. Andy was concerned the cops might have a guy staking out the place, but after careful consideration, he was convinced there was no one watching. To his amazement, when he entered the courtyard, his Harley was still where he had left it. Maybe his belongings were still in his room, too. Then it dawned on him that he didn't have a key. Had the cops taken it? Or did he not have a chance to grab it when he was being arrested? He couldn't honestly remember.

He would have to ask the desk clerk and hope they were not going to be difficult with him. He walked into the front office.

"Can I help you?" asked the lady at the front desk.

"I need a replacement key. I locked my other one in my room," explained Andy.

"What room?" she asked.

"Room 27," he replied.

"Got I.D.?" she asked.

"No, it's in the room too," Andy said. "I can give you my name and how many days I was booked in for. You would probably have a copy of my driver's license on your system, too."

The front desk clerk tapped away at her keyboard.

"Okay. What's the name?" she asked.

"Andy Harlan. H.A.R.L.A.N.," Andy said.

She tapped away at her keyboard some more.

"Can you give me your home address, please?" she asked.

Andy recited it to her. Finally, after some more tapping, she gave him a new key card.

"Try not to lose this one," she said.

"I'll do my best," said Andy. In reality, he planned to grab his stuff and get out of there before any more sheriffs came looking for him.

Chapter Eleven

Andy exited the front office. He was about to head up the stairs to his room when he saw the vending machines. He needed food. He raced up the stairs to his room and checked his belongings. His wallet was still there, hidden in his dresser drawers where he had left it after his night of drinking. He grabbed a bunch of dollar bills and ran back downstairs. He got two packets of potato chips from one machine and an ice-cold soda from the other. He guzzled half the soda before he made it back to his room.

He popped open one bag of chips and ate them in seconds. He looked out the motel window; the sun was setting. It would be dark soon. He needed a shower and a shave before he headed home. He was caked in dirt and filth from his canyon escapades. He grabbed the motel wardrobe and dragged it to the front door. It wouldn't stop an assault team, but it might give him time to pull on his jeans and boots if it came to that.

Satisfied that the door would be difficult to open, he stripped down and jumped in the shower. The warm water and soap on his skin felt amazing. He really did need it. He would probably have to tape up both his small toes when he got home; he had bad blisters on both sides.

It felt good to get into clean clothes again. Andy tossed his prison scrubs and slip-on shoes in the motel room trash can and started to gather his belongings. It was fully dark now. Andy grabbed a fresh pair of socks and marveled at how great they felt. Not enough people in this world appreciate a great pair of socks these days. These felt like heaven on earth to his poor, abused feet. He then pulled on his well-worn engineer boots, a welcome relief from those flimsy jailhouse sneakers. He shoved everything into his backpack, did one last dummy check of his room, including the bathroom, to make sure he didn't leave anything behind, and made his way to the front door. He pulled the wardrobe out of the way and took a look through the peephole. No SWAT team waiting for him just outside the door.

Satisfied the coast was clear, Andy exited his room and headed downstairs. He planned to do a quick dummy check of his bike, make sure no one had tampered with it since his ordeal, and get the hell out of Dodge. There was no way he was coming "home" ever again. He was done with this place.

Andy looked over his Harley. Everything seemed in good shape. No nuts had rattled loose since his last ride, and it didn't appear the cops had messed with either his clutch or brake cables. Maybe they hadn't figured out that the motorcycle was his?

He checked his rear tire. Pressure seemed good. No one had shoved a knife into it or deflated it. Andy was bending over to check his front tire when a sharp pain went across the backs of his legs. Confused, he collapsed to the ground as his legs gave out from under him. It took him a second to realize it was a police-issued billy club.

Chapter Twelve

Stunned, Andy instinctively rolled out of the way just as the billy club came crashing down to his left. He had barely avoided it. It was only then that he realized it was that fat fuck Sheriff Eli Brantley. In pain, Andy struggled to get to his feet.

The Sheriff must have split off from his deputies at some point during their hunt and had been waiting for Andy.

"Where's my nephew, you piece of shit? What did you do to him?" snarled the Sheriff.

Andy squared off against the Sheriff. Fists versus a billy club. He had the advantage of being younger and in better shape, but he was not taking any chances.

"He's dead. I never touched him. A flash flood got him," Andy replied.

"Bullshit, you lying scum!" raged Sheriff Eli.

"The coroner's report will prove I am telling the truth," countered Andy, bracing for the next attack.

As predicted, Sheriff Brantley swung at Andy again. Ready this time, Andy easily stepped out of the way of the billy club. He then rushed in and grabbed the lawman's shirt.

"Listen, you dumb bastard. I never touched your boy."

Brantley struggled against Andy's grip on his uniform. He tried to move his right arm back as Andy used his forearms to keep it pinned.

With a show of strength (and sheer body mass), Sheriff Brantley pushed back against Andy. Andy, using the Sheriff's own body weight against him, swung the Sheriff around and, while aiming to slam him into the wall, sent the portly sheriff right through the windows of the ground-floor motel room that they were fighting in front of. Just in that split second, Andy prayed there was currently no one in that room. Brantley fell to the floor inside the room, crying out in pain. Knocking a few hanging shards out of his way and making sure he wouldn't cut himself, Andy stepped inside the deserted motel room.

Sheriff Eli was cut up, but from what Andy could tell, nothing overly serious.

He bent down and grabbed the Sheriff by his shirt collar.

"Listen, you fat fuck. I never touched your nephew. The coroner's report will show I am not lying. However, I am telling you now, for your own safety, pack your shit and get out of this town. If I ever see you again, I promise I will cut off both your hands and feet. You understand me?"

Andy had no intention of ever coming back or even hacking off the man's appendages. He had been so badly treated by this guy and his goons that he was speaking out of pure pent-up aggression and rage.

"I, I, I," whimpered Sheriff Brantley.

Andy cracked the blubbering Sheriff with a straight right to the jaw, knocking the downed cop out.

It was time to leave before looky-loos, reinforcements, or worse arrived.

Andy started up his Harley. He was just about to pull his helmet on when he felt what seemed like a revolver jammed up against the back of his head. Instinctively, he raised his hands into the "don't shoot" position. He was screwed. No getting out of it this time.

Chapter Thirteen

"Now take it easy there," a semi-familiar voice said to him. Andy knew the voice but couldn't place it.

"Easy, easy," Andy said. "I'm going to turn around slowly."

Andy turned around. He saw a man in his mid-50s with a revolver pointed at him. Who was this guy? It took him a second. He was the motel clerk who had checked him in two days ago.

"What have you done to my windows?" the man asked.

"Look. I'm really sorry," said Andy. "I will pay for the damages."

"What did you throw through there?" asked the motel owner, half peering into the vacant room and half keeping an eye on Andy in case he rushed him.

"Uhhh, the Sheriff was attacking me. It was an accident. Okay?" Andy replied.

"Wait. You put Sheriff Brantley through the window?" asked the desk clerk.

"Uh... yes?" said Andy.

The man lowered his pistol.

"Listen, man, grab your shit and go. Don't worry, leave this with me. We will take care of it."

"So, I'm free to leave?" asked Andy incredulously.

"Yeah! Go," said the motel operator. "You did us a favor. He and his creepy nephew. No one in this town likes them. They would bring drunk girls here and take advantage of them."

Andy thought for a moment. That tracked. This sheriff saw this town as his own personal kingdom to do whatever he wanted.

"You sure?" asked Andy.

"Yeah. I'm sure. Just get out of here. Safe travels, stranger," said the clerk.

"Oh shit. Here's my key. Thanks, man. Much appreciated."

Andy pulled on his helmet, mounted his Harley, and kicked it into first gear. He gave the clerk one last wave before pulling out of the motel. He turned and headed east toward Sedona. One thing was for sure. He had no intentions of coming back to Blackwood Ridge any time soon.

Ghosts of the Iron Hotel

The old Desert Crown Hotel sat three miles off Highway 92, a cracked monument of sun-bleached stucco and shattered windows. They said it once hosted movie stars back in the '50s; now it just hosted ghosts, coyotes, and the occasional drifter.

David "Reaper" Malone rolled up on his Harley as the sun dropped behind the Mule Mountains, dust swirling around his boots. Twenty years in the Iron Nomads had left him with more scars than memories, and prison had taken the rest. Now, at sixty-three, all he wanted was quiet. The hotel's owner, a Tucson developer, offered him a simple deal: live on-site, keep vandals away until the renovation crew arrived in a few weeks. Room and board, cash weekly.

Sounded like peace.

He made himself a little home in one of the old staff rooms. Ate canned beans, drank whiskey, and patrolled the hallways with a flashlight and a .38 tucked in his waistband. Nights were long and dry, filled with the hum of desert wind through broken glass.

On the fifth night, he spotted movement in the ballroom.

At first, he thought it was a coyote; then his flashlight found a woman and a boy huddled near a pile of blankets and a propane stove. The woman looked mid-thirties, lean, eyes sharp as cut glass. The kid couldn't have been more than ten.

"What the hell are you doin' here?" David asked, his voice rough like gravel.

She stood between him and the boy. "We're not hurting anyone. Just need a roof. It's cold out there."

David rubbed his jaw. "This place ain't yours. Ain't mine either. But tomorrow you're movin' on. Can't have you here when the crew comes."

She nodded slowly, eyes dark but understanding. "We'll go in the morning."

David turned, flashlight beam trembling slightly from the ache in his hand. He told himself it was the right thing; rules were rules.

That night, around 2 a.m., the sound of motorcycles split the silence. David felt his stomach sink. The low rumble was too familiar. He stepped outside and saw the colors: Dead Sons MC. Rival club. Old enemies.

Before he could grab his gun, they were on him, three shadows from the past. The leader, Spike, grinned under the flicker of his headlight. "Ain't this somethin'. Reaper Malone, guarding hotels for rich folks. You fell far, brother."

David tried to fight, but age and whiskey slowed him down. They knocked him to the dirt, boots and fists raining down until everything went black.

When he woke, he was inside, the woman kneeling beside him, cleaning his face with a damp rag. The boy hovered nearby, holding a cracked flashlight like it was a sword.

"Easy," she whispered. "You're lucky they didn't kill you."

David groaned, tasting blood. "Should've let 'em try."

She shook her head. "You've had enough trying, old man."

For three days, she nursed him. The boy brought him water and helped clean his wounds. David didn't ask where she learned to stitch a gash that clean or why her hands didn't shake. Maybe she'd been running from her own ghosts.

When he could finally stand again, he found her in the lobby packing her things.

"You don't have to go," he said, voice low. "Not yet. Those Dead Sons won't be back."

She gave him a long look. "We all gotta keep moving, David. You know that."

He watched as she and the boy disappeared down the road, the desert wind kicking dust around their footprints until they were gone.

That night, David sat on the cracked hotel steps, a bottle in hand and his old gun beside him. For the first time in years, he didn't feel like a ghost guarding ruins. Someone had seen him , really seen him , and patched him back together.

When the wind blew, he swore he could still hear the boy's voice echo through the halls.

And in the distance, under a blood-red Arizona sky, a Harley's engine fired up.

David smiled through his busted lip and whispered,

"Still ridin', huh?"

The night answered with silence.

Two Riders Down

Chapter 1 – The Stunt Kings

Mick "Ironhand" Russo and Johnny Vega had been friends since elementary school, growing up in Greenpoint, Brooklyn. Mick's dad bought him a little Honda Grom right after his mom abandoned the family. He and Johnny would take turns riding up and down the block until Johnny's folks finally had enough money to buy him a Grom too. He got a cheap second-hand one, and out of necessity, they both learned to do their own repairs on their little bikes.

Pretty much after that, school was a washout. Why bother studying when all you wanted to do was ride your scooter up and down the neighborhood? Greenpoint back then wasn't gentrified yet, and there were plenty of empty streets and abandoned buildings to explore. Once Johnny got his bike, they would ride all day, only coming home in the evenings for dinner.

In junior high, they decided to be outlaws. Well, that was the goal. After a few minor arrests for dumbass petty crimes, Mick and Johnny realized they weren't cut out for the criminal lifestyle. While they both detested day jobs and "bowing down to the man," they hated jail time even more. They wanted freedom, and jail was the polar opposite of freedom. So a new plan was needed. All their friends were heading off to trade schools or colleges, and they were still just wrenching on their bikes and tearing around the neighborhood. Admittedly, they had upgraded from the Groms they started with to Honda Rebels, and then, of course, Harleys, but yeah, still hanging out, working on their bikes, and riding around the city like madmen.

And just like that, it came to them. One Saturday afternoon, they were fooling around near the waterfront. Back in those days, the Brooklyn Waterfront on weekends was like no man's land. All the factories and warehouses were closed, and you could ride for miles without seeing another soul. But Mick and Johnny did see some guys, a couple of teenagers, much like them, but from Astoria, Queens. While Greenpoint was the northwest tip of Brooklyn, Astoria was the northwest tip of Queens. These guys were riding dirt bikes and had set up a makeshift jump ramp using an old warehouse door propped up. Mick and Johnny were curious.

They pulled over and watched for about ten minutes before introducing themselves. Their Harleys were too heavy and had no chance of standing up to the punishment of stunt riding.

The two guys from Queens, Keith and Jim, offered to let Mick and Johnny try out their dirt bikes. Soon, they were both channeling their inner Evel Knievel and doing jumps. The friends were hooked. After that day, they both vowed to buy dirt bikes.

The problem was money. No money, plus no desire to get jobs, and very few job prospects anyway. So what to do? Mick knew some punk rockers who lived in a squat in Williamsburg (try doing that these days). They planned to buy an ounce of weed, break it into dime bags, and sell it to high school students. With those profits, they would buy a pound of weed and sell it to more high school kids. With that, they could buy dirt bikes and still keep their Harleys.

Spider, a punk rocker living in a squat on North 6th Street, Williamsburg, put Mick and Johnny in touch with a one-percent biker from a club called the Wappinger Wolves. The biker gave them a good deal on the ounce and a pager number (this was long before everyone had cell phones). Inspired, the boys decided to hit high schools in Astoria, Queens, since they were too well-known among the locals in Greenpoint.

Within two months, the boys had turned their initial investment of a few hundred bucks into a money-making scheme. They finally had enough to buy two brand-new dirt bikes from a motorcycle shop on Northern Boulevard in Queens, plus some safety gear, chest protectors, back protectors, stuff they normally didn't bother with when riding their cruisers around. They were in business.

First, they had to master their new bikes. They started with the basics: standing up and riding, learning to use their front brake and feather the back brake. Next, they practiced full-lock figure-eight turns, going as slow as possible. Mick figured they must have done thousands of these in the next year.

Once they were confident in those basics, they started pushing themselves to master wheelies and tabletop jumps. Of course, they dropped or crashed their bikes a lot during this time. In hindsight, they would have been better off buying some used dirt bikes. Oh well, hindsight is 20/20. Regardless, they soon got really good. Local kids would turn up on Saturday afternoons to their makeshift stunt show and cheer them on.

One day, they were back at the motorcycle shop on Northern Boulevard, where they bought their dirt bikes, and the owner approached them. He had a big bike show out on Long Island, and his stunt team had bailed on him. Would they want to do it? $500 each.

Of course, the pair agreed immediately. That was how their professional, death-defying motorcycle act started.

Chapter 2 – Old Debts, New Trouble

From that day on, in the mid-90s, the boys started charging for their stunt show. They soon attracted attention from nationwide motorcycle promoter Lyle Henderson. Starting the season in Daytona Beach, Florida, to Bisbee, Arizona, Laconia, New Hampshire, the granddaddy of them all, Sturgis in South Dakota, and ending each November in Galveston, Texas, with the Lone Star Rally, the pair would travel around the nation wowing the crowd with their dirt bike prowess.

Lyle had loaned them the cash to purchase a used but good-quality RV and trailer, which they soon decked out with their sponsors' logos. After each show, the boys would get paid by Lyle, then, in turn, they would give a large portion of their fee back to him to pay off their debt. Mick always preferred doing it this way so there would be no shenanigans from Lyle. He had heard how shady some promoters could be, and he never wanted to get burned.

After a somewhat successful stunt show in Flagstaff, Arizona, Mick and Johnny went to get paid. They approached Lyle's trailer and knocked, waiting to hear old man Lyle shout "enter" before they went inside. They may be rough and tumble, but they respected a man's office.

After a bit of small talk with the boys, Lyle started counting out their performance fee, then proceeded to hand them a wad of notes.

More out of habit than lack of trust, Mick started to count the money. There was a problem: their agreed-upon fee was significantly short.

"What's this?" asked Mick.

"What do you mean?" asked Lyle. "It's your gig fee."

"There's a problem?" asked Johnny.

"Yeah, there is a problem. You are about two thousand short," said Mick.

"Hey, what can I say?" Lyle replied. "Attendance was shit. I get paid less, I pay you less. I can't give you what I don't have."

Mick swore under his breath. Johnny looked over with a facial expression of "What are we gonna do here?"

"Lyle, c'mon, man. We gotta get our full pay," said Mick. "We have bills to pay."

"Speaking of, I need your RV payment, boys. The loan company is on my back."

"You're kidding, aren't you?" snapped Mick. "How are we meant to pay for the RV on this?" shaking the fistful of dollar bills at Lyle.

"You signed the loan agreement, boys, you gotta pay," Lyle replied.

"For fuck's sake," swore Johnny.

Mick started counting out the cash again, making little mental calculations as he counted.

"Okay, here is what we can afford to pay you, Lyle," said Mick, handing over a small stack of bills.

"What's this?" asked Lyle, as if Mick had just handed him a dog turd.

"That's our loan repayment," said Mick with a sly smile on his face.

"Boys, are you retarded?" exclaimed Lyle. "This won't even cover the interest owed."

"That's all we can afford, Lyle," said Mick.

Lyle pocketed the money and shook his head. "Boys, you are gonna have to make a bigger payment next weekend, or the repo men will probably come after you. I can only do so much."

"What's next weekend?" asked Johnny.

Mick pulled out a battered piece of paper.

"Ah, next weekend is Scottsdale. That's always a big money earner. Right, Lyle?"

"Yeah, should be," said Lyle. "Should be."

"Okay then," said Mick. "We will make up the shortfall after Scottsdale. Alright, Lyle?"

"Sounds good to me, boys," said Lyle. He stood up and shook both their hands, indicating it was time for them to leave.

As they were walking down the steps of Lyle's trailer, they ran face-first into one of the event organizers.

"Oh, hey, boys. Everything okay in there?" asked the man.

"Yeah, all hunky-dory. Why do you ask?" said Johnny.

"Oh, I heard shouting," the man replied.

"Ah, just a simple misunderstanding," said Mick. "We are all good now."

"Very well then," said the man, turning and walking away from Lyle's trailer.

The pair watched the man scurry off to stick his nose in someone else's business.

"So, what do you think?" asked Johnny.

"About what? That guy?" asked Mick.

"No. Scottsdale next weekend!" said Johnny.

"It's the Iron Horizons Chopper Fest. One of the biggest bike shows in the nation. No way can it fail," said Mick with confidence.

Chapter 3 – Blood in the Office

"So, what do you think?" asked Johnny once they were back in their RV.

Mick handed Johnny a beer from their fridge.

"About Scottsdale?" asked Mick. "Yeah. We should be good. That's one of the bigger biker fests in the nation. No way will Lyle lose money on that event. We will make more cash, pay him what we owe him, and have plenty in our pockets."

"Yeah. That's what I reckon too," said Johnny, sipping on his beer.

The boys sat in their lounge, drinking beers and shooting the shit till about 2 a.m. Tomorrow, they would pack all their gear up and make the short two-hour drive down to Scottsdale before the following weekend's biker fest. They had a day off on Monday and Tuesday; they would be on site to supervise the stunt course and jump ramps, a task they had done a hundred times before.

Mick was in a deep sleep when he heard someone pounding on the door to their RV.

What time was it? The sun hadn't even come up yet. Maybe some chicks who wanted to party with him and Johnny? He pulled on a T-shirt and staggered from the back of their RV to the door. To his disappointment, he could see it was a dude. He unlocked the RV door and stuck his head out.

"What time is it?" he slurred, barely awake.

"Dude, grab your shit. Grab Johnny, grab your shit, and get out of here. I figure you have five minutes," said the man.

"Huh? What?" Mick realized it was one of the crew for Lyle's traveling shows, Ohio Tommy.

"Tommy, what are you talking about?" groaned Mick. It was too early for this nonsense.

"The cops are looking for you and Johnny," said Ohio Tommy. "Grab your Harleys and get out of here. I can take care of your RV. I'll text ya when the coast is clear."

"Is this a prank, bro?" asked Mick.

"No. I'm serious," snapped Tommy. "Look." He grabbed Mick and pulled him away from the RV. On the other side of the festival grounds, Mick could see a bunch of police cars and people.

"This has got to be some huge mistake," said Mick to Tommy.

"Maybe so. But you know how cops are. Even if you're innocent, they will railroad you into something just to save face. Grab Johnny, jump on your Harleys, and hit the road. I'll cover for you both."

Shit. Ohio Tommy was serious. Mick kept his nose clean, but he didn't trust the cops. Sure, there were some good ones, but he had been railroaded a couple of times as a teenager and wasn't taking any chances. They could bounce down to Phoenix now, wait until whatever was going on with Lyle had calmed down, and come back later in the day.

"Thanks, Tommy. I'm gonna grab Johnny, and we will slip out the west gate. Text me when it all dies down, would ya?"

"No sweat, bro," said Ohio Tommy. "You guys are my boys. I got your back."

Mick ran back into the RV. He shook Johnny awake and told him to get dressed. He pulled on his jeans and boots and grabbed his leather jacket.

"Let's go, bro. Cops are a-coming!" said Mick.

Johnny was half-dressed.

"Gimme a second, Mick," said Johnny, looking for his wallet. "What the hell is going on?"

"Sounds like Lyle got into a fight with someone. Tommy says the cops are looking for us," explained Mick.

"Fuck that. I hate cops," said Johnny. "Let's hit the road."

They had their riding gear and their wallets. Everything else would be safe, locked up in their RV. Mick was glad they had stashed their stunt bikes after the show last night. Just their Harleys were parked by the large recreational vehicle.

They rolled out of the west gate and weaved through the early morning streets, looking for the road to take them to the freeway that would lead them south to Phoenix.

Chapter 4 – Framed and Hunted

Mick and Johnny were close to the halfway point to Phoenix when the sun started poking up over the mountains on their left. Mick saw the signs for a roadside diner and signaled to Johnny that they should pull over. The pair had been traveling the road together for so long now that they understood each other's myriad of hand signals, even if no one else did.

The diner was a few blocks past the freeway. Mick always preferred the diners connected to the freeway. You pull off, get your food, hit the restroom, and swing back on and continue your journey. These ones that lead you left, then right, turn here, turn there, you never knew if you were ever going to find your way back again.

Two miles off the freeway, they finally found the diner. It certainly looked promising. A mom-and-pop-run diner versus a cookie-cutter chain restaurant. Usually, the food in these was fresher, cheaper, and in bigger portions than you got at the chains. Mick was hopeful. There was no parking out front, so they cruised down the alley and ended up finding a safe spot to park their bikes near the back of the restaurant.

The food was actually good, and the coffee helped Mick wake up. He had been riding for about an hour but was almost on automatic pilot. After coffee, he could think clearly. He was grateful to Tommy for having their back and giving them a chance to get up before the cops grabbed them. The last thing he or Johnny needed today was to spend eight hours in the cop station getting "interviewed," only to be let go after they realized the pair was not the guys they were looking for. Whatever beef Lyle had going on, Mick was confident it would be resolved by the afternoon. They could go back, collect their RV, and head back to Phoenix.

After they had finished their morning feast, Mick made the gesture to the waitress that they needed the check. Sure enough, all that food came to under twenty bucks for two people. Not too many places were left in America where you could get two breakfasts for under twenty bucks. He made a mental note to remember this place so they could hit it next time they traveled this stretch of road.

The waitress told them they had to settle up at the cashier's desk near the entrance to the restaurant. As they were standing in line to pay, two local cops walked in, ignored them, and went and grabbed a booth. Mick was sure glad they were having no issues with law enforcement today.

As they waited to pay their check, the TV behind the cashier's desk droned on and on. Mick casually listened in, somewhat ignoring the boring newscasters' stories as they droned on.

Then he heard it.

"The police are looking for two outlaw bikers wanted for questioning for the murder of popular motorcycle festival promoter LYLE HENDERSON."

It was like time stood still. All Mick could focus on was the television above the woman's head.

Lyle? Murdered? What? By who?

The cashier reached out to grab Mick's check. Without taking his eyes off the TV set, he mindlessly handed her their bill.

Lyle had been robbed, his throat slit, continued the newscaster. Two bikers who worked with Lyle were last seen leaving his trailer after a vicious argument, explained the newsreader.

Mick thought it over. What two bikers would do such a thing? Sure, Lyle was a cantankerous old coot, but that was no reason for anyone to kill him.

"That will be eighteen dollars, please," said the cashier. There was a line of customers waiting to pay, standing behind Johnny.

Mick was glued to the TV set.

"Eighteen dollars, please, sir," the cashier insisted.

"Hey, hurry up and pay, would ya?" someone shouted from behind Johnny. Mick realized he was holding up the line. He grabbed a stack of money that Lyle had handed them yesterday and counted out enough to cover their bill and a tip.

The lady counted out the money, hit some buttons on the register, and slid the bills into their rightful drawers. Mick was still transfixed by the TV set.

The last thing the newscaster said was that the two bikers in question had fled the scene, and law enforcement was on the lookout for them. Johnny was grabbing Mick and dragging him out of the store.

"You think Tommy is in on it?" asked Johnny.

"What do you mean? He killed Lyle? No way, bro. He loved that old fart," Mick replied.

"No, dude. Think," said Johnny as they walked the alley behind the diner to get to their Harleys.

"What?" asked Mick.

"You think he set us up?" asked Johnny.

"Wait, what?" asked Mick. It was dawning on him. The two bikers that the news report alluded to were THEM!

"You think people think we did it?" asked Mick, aghast.

"Dude. C'mon," said Johnny. "Two bikers were last seen leaving his trailer! That nerd who cornered us when we left Lyle, remember?"

"Oh, fuck. No way. We didn't do shit," Mick replied.

"I know that! I was there with you, remember?" said Johnny.

"So what should we do? Turn ourselves in?" asked Mick.

"We have already run, bro. We come back now, they'll probably shoot us first and ask questions later," said Johnny.

"Damn that Tommy," cursed Mick.

"Well, he probably thought he was doing us a solid," said Johnny.

"Yeah, true," said Mick. "So what should we do?"

"I reckon let's head to Phoenix and lay low until they catch the real killers," suggested Johnny. "Easier to fly under the radar there than some small town."

"Yeah, good call," said Mick. "Let's get moving before those two cops inside start searching for us."

The duo took off and headed south towards Phoenix.

Part II
On the Run

Chapter 5 – Road to Nowhere

The pair had the best intentions of heading to Phoenix, riding hard and as fast as possible without drawing law enforcement's attention. They were close to approaching the town of Anthem, the first sign of civilization as you made your way to Phoenix, when they saw it. Police roadblock about two miles ahead. Was it for them? Who could tell? Who wanted to find out? Just at the last minute, Mick spied a small off-ramp for the town of Red Mesa. He gestured to Johnny that they needed to pull off, and luckily, Johnny recognized right away what Mick was saying. If they got through this, they would really have to think about investing in Cardo packs so they could talk to each other via their helmets.

As they followed the small two-lane road towards the town of Red Mesa, Mick remembered he had a friend who lived out this way, Five Fingers Frankie. Frankie got his name as a kid growing up in Brooklyn because he could literally shoplift any item. Mick recalled that he once went to a sporting goods store and stole a wetsuit and spear gun without breaking a sweat. Frankie was finally caught when he turned eighteen. He did a short stretch in some upstate New York prison, and when he got out, he left New York for the Southwest for a fresh start. If anyone could help them now, it would be Frankie.

They were now far enough away from the I-17 freeway that Mick felt confident enough they were safe to pull over. He signaled Johnny, and they found a patch off the shoulder that was wide enough for them to stop without getting flattened by an eighteen-wheeler.

"What are we doing here?" asked Johnny.

"I have a friend who lives near here. Well, you know him. Frankie from Bushwick," said Mick.

"Frankie lives out here?" asked Johnny.

"Yeah. Don't you remember? He moved out here for a fresh start," said Mick. "Gimme a minute, gonna try and call him."

Mick was surprised he got a phone signal this far from civilization. He dialed Frankie's number, and it rang. A familiar voice picked up.

"Hello? Who's this?" asked Frankie.

"Frankie, it's Mick."

"Which Mick? I know a lot of Micks," Frankie replied, forever cautious.

"Greenpoint Mick," said Mick. "Ironhand."

"Oh shit, man. Listen carefully. Mile marker 32, there's a dirt road, follow it out for about two miles. Blue house on the right."

"Wait, what?" asked Mick.

"Mile marker 32, dirt road, blue house. Bye," and just like that, Frankie hung up.

WTF? thought Mick. That was rude.

Mick explained to Johnny how the conversation with Frankie had gone. Johnny didn't seem too fussed, and they decided the best thing they could do was get right to Frankie's place and speak to him face to face.

They continued heading west, keeping a sharp eye out for mile markers. 29, 30, 31, and there it was, mile marker 32. Mick waved to Johnny and blipped down through the gears to make the turn onto the dirt road, half expecting his back wheel to slide out. Nope, it held fast.

They were now heading north again. Just nothing but them, a million cactus, and some tumbleweeds. Good Lord, Frankie was a long way away from the gritty streets of Bushwick. After a few more twists and turns, ups and downs along this old dirt road, Mick finally spotted the blue house. There were no other houses as far as the eye could see. Frankie could have just as easily said the house on the right; it wasn't like the street was lined with multiple dwellings. How on earth Frankie ended up here, Mick didn't know, but let's just say if there was ever a zombie apocalypse, then Frankie should do okay.

Before they had even pulled up, Frankie came running out of his place. I guess out here, any noise, any car or bike, and you are going to hear it, figured Mick. Frankie hadn't changed much; his hair was a little grayer near his temples, but otherwise he looked exactly as Mick remembered him.

Frankie was instructing them to take their bikes around the back of his place. Like, who was going to be driving along this godforsaken road and spot them? Regardless, Mick and Johnny followed his directions and parked in an empty barn around the back of his property.

As soon as they had parked and shut off their Harleys, Frankie hugged them both.

"C'mon, quick. Get inside," he instructed. Without asking, the pair followed Frankie inside his place. It was a small, simple house, barely furnished, but the first thing that struck Mick was that the curtains were drawn on every window. It was not like ol' Frankie had any nosy neighbors.

"Whoa. Why all the secrecy?" asked Johnny after Frankie had shut the back door.

"Oh, you guys don't know?" asked Frankie.

"Know what?" asked Mick.

"You're all over the news. Every law enforcement agency in the state is looking for you both."

Mick's heart sank. They were screwed.

Chapter 6 – The New Names

"We're screwed," announced Johnny, almost as if he was reading Mick's mind.

"Ye of little faith," said Frankie. "Why give up so soon?"

"You just said every cop in the state is looking for us," exclaimed Johnny.

"So? You lay low until you figure out how to clear your names," shrugged Frankie.

"Easier said than done," Mick replied.

"Anything is possible if you put your mind to it," Frankie said.

"Again, that's easy for you to say," Mick replied.

"Oh shit. I'm sorry, guys. Forgive me," said Frankie. "I never offered you a refreshing beverage. I've got beers or soda. Take your pick."

"I'll take a beer," said Johnny.

"Sure, why not," said Mick, plonking himself down on Frankie's sectional couch.

Frankie returned with three beers and handed one to each of the boys. They made small talk, catching up on the last few years. After getting out of prison, Frankie felt that he was "known" to the Brooklyn Police Department and would never get fair treatment from them. He left the East Coast and headed out to the Southwest to start again. After a year of living and working in Phoenix, he felt it was best to move far away from civilization, and that's how he ended up living out in the desert near the town of Red Mesa.

"So what should we do?" asked Johnny.

"I say lay low and let me reach out to my contacts and see if I can get to the bottom of this," suggested Frankie.

"Lay low? We probably have one hundred bucks between us. How the hell are we gonna lay low with a hundred bucks?" asked Mick.

Frankie thought for a moment. "Here, come with me."

He led the pair into one of the spare rooms off the side of the living room. It looked like a photographer's studio.

"What's all this?" asked Mick.

"The solution to half your problems," smiled Frankie.

"I didn't get it," said Johnny.

"I make fake IDs as a side hustle," explained Frankie. "It won't get you on a plane, but it will pass most checks."

"Oh shit. We can't afford those," said Mick.

"Eh, you guys probably don't remember it, but you saved my ass from a beatdown in that bar in Williamsburg one night. So consider it a freebie."

"Well damn. Thanks, Frankie," said Johnny.

"How long will this all take?" asked Mick.

Frankie thought for a moment. "Well… no more than ninety minutes, I would guess."

"No shit. That's crazy. Thanks, brother," said Johnny.

"I'm gonna say you boys both live in Phoenix. If you get stopped, they will be looking for two bikers from NYC, not Phoenix," Frankie explained.

"Yeah, good thinking," said Mick.

Frankie ran them through the process, took their photos, and then told them to grab more beers and go hang out in the living room. They kicked back on the couch and watched the news, which went on and on about poor Lyle's murder.

Finally, Frankie came out of his photo lab.

"Ta-da!" he announced. "Here ya go, boys. My finest work, if I say so myself."

Frankie handed Mick and Johnny their new driver's licenses.

"Ray? Ray Delgado?" asked Johnny.

"Sure, why not?" asked Frankie. "You got a problem with that?"

"No, no. No problem. What did you get, Mick?" asked Johnny.

"Jack. Jack Stevens," said Mick.

"Damn. That's cool," exclaimed Johnny.

"Like I said," said Frankie. "These should get by most traffic cops, but just don't try to get on a plane with them."

"What's this address in Phoenix?" asked Mick.

"Oh, that's an apartment building up the street from a famous biker bar, 'The Filthy Hogg.' The building is real; the apartment number doesn't exist."

"Ah, good thinking, Frankie," said Mick. "I gotta say, we owe ya big time."

"Nah, we are good, brother," said Frankie.

"So what's the plan?" asked Johnny.

"I say head to town. It's a couple of miles west of here," said Frankie. "Get a motel and lay low a couple of days and let me figure out what's going on."

"Okay, but we ain't got any money," said Mick.

Frankie disappeared and came back with a handful of dollar bills.

"I reckon I've got about two hundred here," said Frankie. "You guys are welcome to it. Just pay me back once you clear your names."

"Damn, brother. You are too kind," said Mick, pocketing the crumpled-up bills.

"In the meantime, I'll make some calls," said Frankie. "Actually, thinking about it, take this burner phone."

Frankie handed Mick a cheap flip phone, the kind you could pick up for $20 from a dollar store.

"Gimme your cell phones," said Frankie.

"For what?" asked Johnny.

"You gotta dump your SIM cards. They can probably track you using those," Frankie explained.

Mick and Johnny quickly popped the backs off their phones and slipped out their SIM cards.

"Okay, don't put 'em back in until I give ya the green light. You understand?" asked Frankie.

"Yes, Dad," said Johnny.

"Ha ha. Very funny. I'm serious. They can track ya with those in," said Frankie.

"Thanks, brother. We definitely owe ya," said Mick. "Is there anything else we should know before we get out of here?"

"Hmm. Not really. Just lay low and keep out of trouble," said Frankie. "Oh, wait. Actually, there is one more thing. Don't stay at the 'Haunted' hotel in town. It's a tourist trap and overpriced. On the west side of town, there is a Moto Lodge or an Auto Lodge or something. Stay there. Just as good, but a quarter of the price."

"Okay, noted. Thanks, Frankie," said Mick.

"There's actually a biker bar within walking distance of the motel," said Frankie. "Blood and Chrome Saloon or something."

"We will keep an eye out for it," said Mick, grabbing his riding gear.

"I've got the number for that phone. So if it ever rings, you should know it's probably me. But be cautious just in case, ya know?" said Frankie.

"Will do," said Johnny.

Frankie walked them back outside to the barn.

"So yeah, head down that way, and once you get back on the main road, head west," said Frankie.

"Thanks again, brother," said Mick. "Work your magic. We look forward to hearing from ya."

The pair fired up their Harleys and rode back via the long, winding dirt road to the main street again. The two-lane blacktop felt positively modern compared to Frankie's dirt road. Prison must have really screwed up Frankie's head to live alone all the way out there, mused Mick, as they made their way to the town of Red Mesa.

Chapter 7 – Cass the Bartender

About 15 minutes into riding the two-lane, sunburnt blacktop, Mick and Johnny (now "Jack" and "Ray") started to see signs for Red Mesa. Like a lot of Arizona mining towns that had seen better days, Red Mesa had reinvented itself as an artist colony, and there were galleries, coffee shops, and even microbreweries littering Main Street.

Mick spied the signs for the "World's Most Haunted Hotel" and kept riding west down Main Street to see if they could find the Moto Lodge that Frankie had tipped them off about. If that was out of business, they were going to be out of luck fast as far as accommodation was concerned.

Up ahead, Mick spotted the telltale signs of a good biker bar: The Chrome and Smoke Saloon. That must have been the place Frankie had told them about. Hopefully, the motel was still in business, too.

The pair was in luck; they finally found the old motel on the outskirts of town. One room with two beds came in at $45 a night. Mick, now Jack, paid cash for three nights and showed his brand-new driver's license as ID. It passed the motel clerk's scrutiny with flying colors.

They found their ground-floor room with ease and decided to roll both their Harleys inside, one to protect them from potential thieves and two, just in case, law enforcement in Red Mesa were looking for "two bikers."

After chilling in their room for thirty minutes, Mick said to Johnny, "Hey, you wanna go out? Maybe check out that bar back there?"

"Sure, man. I'm going crazy just sitting around in here."

They left their riding gear in their motel room, locked up, and started walking back up Main Street. While most of Red Mesa had seen some form of gentrification, this part of town was still pretty run-down. Two blocks up from their motel, they spied the Chrome and Smoke Saloon. Definitely a biker bar. There were a couple of Harleys parked up front, and even from outside, Mick could hear loud rock blasting on the jukebox.

As they walked in, a couple of old dudes sitting in a booth stopped talking, looked them over, then went back to their conversation. No biggie. Mick would have probably done the same.

They decided to sit up by the bar. There was an attractive bartender covered in tattoos working behind the counter. Mick's interest piqued.

They grabbed two barstools and parked themselves by the counter.

"Afternoon, boys," said the tattooed bartender.

"Afternoon, ma'am. Two Modelos, please," asked Mick.

"You want lime with those?" asked the woman.

Mick looked over at Johnny. Johnny nodded his head.

"One with, one without, please," said Mick.

The woman poured both their beers.

"Here ya go," she said.

"Thanks," said Mick.

Mick and Johnny took a swig each from their glasses. The cold beers tasted good after the stressful day they had been having. Drinking at Frankie's had only whetted their appetites.

"New in town?" asked the bartender.

"Yeah. Up from Phoenix," lied Mick. "Looking for work."

"Phoenix, eh?" asked the bartender.

"Yeah," said Johnny. "My name is Ray, by the way." He held out his hand.

"Hi, I am Cassidy," said the tattooed bartender. "But you can call me Cass."

"Hey, Cass, I'm Jack," lied Mick.

"Jack and Ray. Okay, got it," said Cass. "What sort of work do you do?"

"Work on bikes a lot," said Mick.

"Oh. That's a shame," said Cass. "I was hoping you were going to say construction."

"We also do construction," said Johnny.

Mick could barely hide his surprise at that. The most construction they had done was making launch ramps as teens. Well, Johnny had helped some punk rockers build some skate ramps in an abandoned warehouse in Williamsburg, but that was it as far as woodworking experience.

"Oh, that's cool," said Cass. "Come with me."

"Should we leave our beers?" asked Johnny.

"What? Oh yeah. Leave 'em. They'll be safe here," said Cass.

She led them out the back of the bar into the yard behind the building. There was a huge pile of lumber and a stack of bricks.

"What's all this?" asked Mick.

"We had a couple of guys that were going to build a deck out here so we could have bands play and stuff," explained Cass. "As soon as they got paid their deposit, they took off out of town. Tweakers probably."

"Damn, that sucks," said Mick.

"Yeah, it does," said Cass. "So if you think you are up for it, the job is yours."

Mick looked over at Johnny, who seemed to be doing mathematical calculations in his head.

"We could do it. Probably take us a week, though. That's okay?" asked Johnny.

Cass thought it over. "Hm, sure. Cash okay?" she asked.

"Yeah, that works," said Mick, trying to hide his excitement. Extra cash would tide them over until Frankie found the real killers of poor Lyle.

The trio reentered the bar so that they could finish their beers.

Cass and the boys negotiated a price to build the deck and shook on it.

Mick realized that they hadn't eaten all day, and Cass recommended a cool Mexican place a few blocks away. The duo said their goodbyes and left to get food, promising to come back at 10 a.m. the next morning to get started.

"You sure you know what you are doing?" asked Mick.

"Eh, pretty much," said Johnny.

"Oh shit," said Mick. "I have no clue, so I will just follow along."

"Yeah. No problem," said Johnny. "At least I bought us some time, ya know?"

"Yeah, good thinking, brother. Let's get some food. I am starving."

"Me too," said Johnny.

Chapter 8 – Shadows in the Desert

Mick and Johnny spent the next two days working on the deck for Cass. On top of the cash-in-hand work, she gave them a free meal and beers at night, an added bonus.

Back at their motel, flicking through the TV stations before bed on that second night, Mick came across a news story about the Iron Horizon's Chopper Fest in Scottsdale. Two bikers from New York State had been murdered.

"Whoa! Check this," said Mick.

"Yeah, I heard," said Johnny. "Did you know them?"

"No clue, bro," Mick replied. "That's not the point. The point is, they were from New York."

"Yeah. So?"

"Don't you get it?" asked Mick. "I reckon someone, maybe the killer, thought that was US!"

"Oh shit. Maybe."

"Come on. Has to be," Mick replied.

Chapter 9 – Digging Up Henderson's Past

The next morning, working on Cassidy's outdoor deck, Mick heard his burner flip phone go off. He waved to Johnny that he had to take the call. Johnny stopped working and went to grab some water from the cooler. Sure enough, it was Frankie.

"Can you talk?" asked Frankie.

"Yeah. What ya got for me?" asked Mick.

"The Kane brothers," said Frankie.

"Who?" asked Mick.

"Earl and Travis Kane. Two real scumbags. The word on the street is they are the ones who killed your pal."

"Oh shit. Thanks, Frankie," Mick replied.

"They just killed two dudes in Scottsdale last night, thinking it was you and Johnny."

"I knew it! I fucking knew it," swore Mick.

"There's more," said Frankie.

"Okay."

"The word I am getting from friends in the know is that your buddy Lyle was in deep with an East Coast mob."

"You mean, like …" Mick replied.

"Yeah. Like THAT," said Frankie. "I'm doing my best to get more intel for ya."

"Thanks, brother. We owe ya," said Mick.

"Just stay alert and be wary of any strangers coming to town. If ya get me."

"Yeah. We will. Thanks, Frankie."

Mick hung up and went over to explain the phone call to Johnny. After Mick had told Johnny about the call, the two sat and thought about their situation.

"Look, if we can tie these Kane brothers to the mob, we should be able to clear our names," said Johnny.

"Yeah. I am thinking the same," said Mick.

"Trouble is, how?" asked Johnny.

"I dunno, man. But, you know how these things work. I am sure when the time comes, the solution will reveal itself to us."

"Yeah, you're right, Mick," Johnny replied.

Chapter 10 – Bonds Forged in Dust

That night, after work, the duo sat at the bar hanging out with Cassidy. She was pleased with the progress they'd made on her deck and comped them a couple of beers and dinner.

Mick kept one eye on the door all night, convinced the Kane brothers were going to show up looking for them. Ridiculous, really, he had no idea what they looked like, and they probably didn't know what he and Johnny looked like. Regardless, he stayed vigilant.

Around nine, four bikers walked in. Mick scanned for colors but didn't see anything recognizable. Small, up-and-coming club, maybe? Either way, his gut said they were bad news. He stayed on high alert.

Johnny had taken quite a shine to Cassidy, doing his best to flirt. Mick had long ago learned that bartenders were immune to pick-up lines, but he still enjoyed watching his brother try.

A few more beers in, Mick heard shouting. The bikers had picked a fight with a local guy out with his girlfriend. Mick's blood boiled. Four on one? Weak. The local tried to de-escalate, but one of the bikers blocked his exit.

Mick nudged Johnny. "I'm slipping out the back. Be ready when it kicks off."

"Wait, what?" Johnny asked.

"Ah, never mind. Got ya," Mick replied.

The pair moved instinctively. Johnny positioned himself to watch the front door. The doofus still blocked the exit, and the local was still trying to talk his way out. Johnny waited for Mick.

Time seemed to freeze. The front door swung open, and the dumbass yelped as Mick yanked him outside. His three buddies froze, trying to figure out what had happened. Johnny's cue. In a split second, he tackled the nearest biker, toppling him into his two friends. Chaos erupted.

One biker regained his feet and lunged at Johnny, winding up to punch him, then Mick appeared from outside, putting him in a chokehold and dragging him through the front door.

That left two. Johnny kicked the original biker in the head, sending him sprawling. He leapt over another to land on the last standing foe, sending them both flying out the front door. Mick tossed the downed body of his chokehold victim to the ground. Johnny moved to grab the last troublemaker when the door burst open again. The local had his attacker in a headlock, dragging him outside. Johnny laughed. One-on-one, they weren't so tough.

Mick, Johnny, and the locals squared off against the bloodied bikers. "Get out of town, assholes!" shouted Johnny.

"And don't come back!" shouted the local.

The four out-of-towners scrambled to their Harleys and roared off. Satisfied, the trio headed back inside.

"You guys okay?" Mick asked.

"Yeah. A little bruised but worth it," Johnny smiled.

"Hey, thanks for that," said the local. "My name's Keith."

"No worries, man. I hate bullies," Mick said, shaking his hand. "I'm Jack, and this is Ray."

Cassidy was surprised to see everyone walk back in relatively intact.

"Wow. You guys okay?"

"Yeah, all good here," Mick smiled.

"All in a day's work," Johnny laughed.

Cassidy poured new drinks, including one for Keith and his girlfriend.

"Thanks for not wrecking my bar," she said.

"Our pleasure," Johnny replied.

Walking back to their motel that night, Mick's flip phone rang. It was Frankie.

"Hey, good news, man," Frankie said.

"What's up? They caught the Kane brothers?" Mick asked.

"Nah. Even better. I got word to my people in Scottsdale to let the Kanes know you two have been spotted in Red Mesa, baiting them."

Mick exhaled slowly. Being bait made him uneasy. What if a snitch tipped off law enforcement?

"Oh shit," he said. "You think they'll be coming?"

"Yeah. Be ready," Frankie said, then hung up.

Chapter 11 – The First Confrontation

Two days had passed since Frankie's call. The boys remained vigilant even while finishing off the deck for Cass's bar. No sign of the Kane brothers whatsoever.

Johnny suggested they try checking out the other popular bar on Main Street, right down the other end. As soon as they walked in, they were told to leave as it was a "family establishment" and didn't serve bikers. A good chance the Kane brothers would not be frequenting the joint.

Cassidy was happy to have Mick and Johnny hang out at the bar despite them finishing work for her. She joked they could be her bouncers. The reality was that if they didn't find more cash in hand work soon, they would probably have to leave town.

Around nine pm, a lone woman came in. Made a noise, looked around the bar, then left. Probably looking for her old man, figured Mick. She seemed to be studying every biker in the place before making her exit.

They had taken to waiting around until closing time before heading back to their motel. God forbid these Kane brothers did anything to poor Cassidy when she was closing up. Mick and Johnny would never be able to forgive themselves.

Cassidy was closing out for the night as Mick and Johnny sipped on their final beers of the night. Mick was in the process of trying to figure out what to do next if the Kanes never showed up when he heard it. The unmistakable roar of two Harleys coming down Main Street. He nudged Johnny. Johnny nodded. He knew the sound, too.

The roar got louder and louder, and then, just like that, it stopped. Mick and Johnny waited. No one came in.

Mick assumed the worst. The biker mama from earlier was probably a friend of the Kanes. She had been sent in to scout the place. They knew Mick and Johnny were inside and waiting for them outside. Maybe it was paranoia, but better to be safe than sorry, eh?

Mick grabbed Johnny.

"Listen. I think they are waiting for us outside. I'm going to go through the front door. Give it a minute, and carefully slip out the back and circle to the front. Be very, very careful. Just in case they have someone waiting in the back alley."

Johnny thought for a minute.

"Sure thing, bro. Be careful, though. I don't need ya getting shot."

"I doubt they will use guns. Seems like they prefer knives. Plus, if they start shooting now, they are going to bring the whole town down on them," Mick replied.

"Yeah, good point, bro. Regardless, be safe. Okay?"

"I will," said Mick, finishing off the rest of his beer before getting off his barstool. He felt oddly calm despite the fact that there was a very good chance he was about to be face-to-face with the two brothers who killed poor Lyle.

Mick pushed the front door of the bar open a crack and peered outside. The street was deserted despite it being just after midnight. Small town living, eh? he thought to himself.

He decided to take the plunge and step outside. He gingerly opened the door and stepped out. Looking to his right, nothing. He turned to his left and found himself face to face with a shotgun shoved in his face.

"Whoa! Easy, easy," he said, raising his hands in the "don't shoot" position.

"You, Mike, or Jimmy?" the voice on the other end of the shotgun asked.

"Mick."

"Whatever," said the voice.

"I assume you're after the rest of Lyle's money?" Mick lied.

"Wait. What?" asked the voice.

"His secret stash," said Mick. "C'mon. Everyone knew about that."

Whichever Kane brother was holding the shotgun on Mick started to lower it.

"How do we find this stash?" asked the man.

"We can take you there," Mick lied.

"Okay..." said the voice.

At that moment, Johnny came flying out of the alleyway, sprinted towards the Kane brothers, and took a flying leap at the man holding the shotgun on Mick. Both went down in a tangle of arms and legs; the shotgun was sent flying across the sidewalk. Mick immediately swung at the other Kane brother, clipping him clean on the chin with his right fist. The man wobbled on his feet, clearly stunned. Mick grabbed hold of the man's filthy flannel shirt, pulled him forward, wrapped his right ankle around the man's right foot, and pushed him back, sending the balding Kane brother down to the street hard. He then leapt on top of the man and unleashed a flurry of blows to the man's face and head.

Across the street, a pickup truck took off. Was that the woman from before? Had she been parked across the street, keeping an eye on the bar? It all happened so fast, Mick didn't have a chance to fully register what type of truck it was.

Johnny had gotten to his feet and was booting the downed Kane brother with his engineer boots. That had to hurt. The man tried to roll out of the way of the onslaught of kicks.

Mick got up off the downed Kane brother and went to retrieve the shotgun. After grabbing it, he pulled Johnny away. Despite the two Kane brothers being complete scumbags, Mick didn't like to see men kicked when they were down.

The two Kane brothers got to their feet. Now the shotgun was pointed at them. The older of the two Kane brothers, the one who was balding, wiped blood away from his mouth.

"Fuck you guys," he snarled.

"Get out of here," shouted Johnny.

The Kane brothers dusted themselves off and started backing up towards their parked Harleys, at no time taking their eyes off Mick and Johnny.

Mick kept the shotgun aimed at the brothers until they had mounted their Harleys and taken off up Main Street. He had no doubt they would be back at some time in the future.

Chapter 12 – Desert Smoke

Cass came out and checked on the boys. Once she was assured they were both all right, she let them back into the bar for a final drink for the night.

Mick and Johnny made sure she was able to get home safely that night and retired to their hotel. The last thing they wanted was for the Kanes to try to attack her on her drive home.

Mick and Johnny returned to the Chrome and Smoke Saloon after the lunchtime rush was over the very next day. They were sitting at the bar chilling when the saloon's phone rang. Cass answered it.

"Hold on. It's for you," she mouthed to Mick.

Mick thought for a moment. Who would be calling him at the bar? Had to be the Kanes. They didn't have his burner phone number. Had to be them. Were they watching the bar now?

He took the phone from Cass.

"Hello?"

"This is Earl. Who am I speaking to?"

"This is Mick. We met last night."

"Ah, okay. So listen. We need that money," said Earl Kane.

"What money?" asked Mick.

"Lyle's secret stash, asshole."

"Ah, that. Yeah, about that," said Mick, remembering his lie from last night. "Let me talk to my partner and see what we can do for you. Can you call back in 30 minutes?"

There was silence on the other end of the phone. Mick assumed Earl was mulling over his options.

"Okay. We will call back in thirty minutes. No funny business, or we'll kill you, your little buddy, and the chick that runs that bar. You understand me?"

Earl hung up. Mick handed the phone back to Cass. She could see something was wrong on his face.

"You okay?" she asked.

"Eh, in a situation," said Mick.

"What's wrong?" she asked. Johnny looked on with concern.

Mick decided it was time to come clean.

"Look, our names are not Jack and Ray. We are Mick and Johnny. I am sorry we lied to you."

Cass smiled. "Yeah, I had the feeling you were the two guys the cops were looking for."

"Look. We're innocent," said Johnny. "Those two guys last night killed our friend and tried to blame us."

"I don't know why. But I trust you both. What are you going to do?" asked Cass.

"I have an idea," Mick explained. "We lure them somewhere, film a confession, and clear our names."

"I like it," said Johnny.

"There's a small abandoned mining town about five miles west of here," said Cass. "Dead Coyote Canyon."

"Hmm. That could work," said Mick. "I assume tourists are around all the time?"

"No, no tourists. It's deserted."

"I like it," said Mick.

Chapter 13 – The Trap Set

True to his word, Earl Kane rang back right at the thirty-minute mark. Cass picked up the phone and passed it over to Mick.

"Well," said Earl.

"This Earl?" asked Mick.

"You know it's me. Quit stalling. You gonna hand over the old man's stash or nah?"

Cassidy slid over a hand-drawn map on a napkin.

"Okay. We are ready to play ball," Mick started. "There's a place called Dead Coyote Canyon a few miles west of here."

"Okay."

"We can meet you, say, 11 a.m. tomorrow and give you the location," Mick explained.

"Why not this afternoon?" asked Earl.

"Well, I have to ride back to Phoenix and get the map," Mick lied. "Right now, I know the general location, but let's face it, the desert is a big place. We need the exact location."

Mick could tell once again Earl was weighing up his options.

"Fine. 11 a.m," Earl eventually replied. "Where?"

Mick studied Cassidy's hand-drawn map.

"Head west down Main Street for five miles, and you will see a sign for the turnoff to Dead Coyote Canyon on your right. We will meet you there. 11 a.m. tomorrow, okay?"

Earl repeated back the directions. "Five miles out of town, turn off the right-hand side. Got it."

"Okay. Cool."

"Just so you know, no games or we kill you, your buddy, and that chick. You understand me?" said Earl.

"Yes. No games. Of course," Mick replied.

"Oh, and come unarmed," Earl added.

"Okay. See you then," said Mick before hanging up.

"Well?" asked Cass after Mick handed back the phone.

"You got any firearms?" asked Mick.

"Sorry, no, I don't."

"We still have their shotgun," said Johnny.

"That piece of crap? Probably more dangerous to bring it than leave it behind," mused Mick.

"So, no weapons?" asked Johnny.

"We are just going to have to survive on our wits."

"So, normal day for us then, eh?" asked Johnny.

"You know it."

"Who's going to film them?" asked Johnny. "Frankie?"

"I doubt it. Even though the Kane brothers are pure evil, Frankie won't have anything to do with helping law enforcement."

"Ugh, true," said Johnny.

"I'll do it," volunteered Cassidy.

"You?" asked Johnny.

"No way," said Mick. "Too dangerous."

"I'll be fine," said Cassidy. "11 a.m., right? I'll just get there an hour or two earlier and find a good place to hide."

"I don't like it," said Mick.

"You don't have much choice, mister," said Cass. "Doesn't seem like you have many other options open to you either."

Mick thought about it for a moment. "Okay, fine. But you have to stay hidden. I don't trust these scumbags one bit."

Cass spent some time sketching out Dead Coyote Canyon and pointing out various landmarks to Mick and Johnny. After that, Mick figured he would have to ride into Phoenix, just in case someone connected to the Kanes was watching the bar. If he didn't leave, there was a good chance they would know about it.

Chapter 14 – Guns, Grit, and Gasoline

Mick made it back from Phoenix by 10 pm. He didn't see any telltale signs that he had been followed there or back, but assumed someone had spotted him and informed the Kanes. That was fine by him. Exactly the sort of distraction he needed to create.

He got a good night's sleep and was ready to roll by 9 am. He figured he would get there early enough and scout out the area around Dead Coyote Canyon before they had to meet the Kanes at 11 am.

After a quick once-over on their Harleys to make sure no bolts had rattled loose, Mick and Johnny were ready to head out. Tucked into his back pocket was a fake map that Cassidy had drawn up. Mick figured it would help extract a confession from the Kanes and also make his story look a bit more believable. This was it. Do or die time. Whatever happens in the next two hours is going to change the course of their lives, for better or for worse. Mick felt a surge of adrenaline that he usually only got right before the start of a stunt show. Of course, once the stunt show was happening, he was fine. It was always those thirty minutes before the stunt show that made him nervous.

The five-mile ride out of town was actually picturesque. It was a shame the ride was going to be ruined by having to face the Kanes in a few hours, but anything to clear their names with law enforcement.

It didn't take long to find the turnoff to the abandoned mining town. The two friends came to a stop at the turnoff. Very few cars were on this stretch of road. Mick shut his bike down.

"We've got ninety minutes before the Kanes get here. Let's get up there and scope out the area and make sure it's all kosher," said Mick.

"Yeah, good call," Johnny replied.

They took off up the dirt road heading north, following the twists and turns as they approached the old town. Mick noticed a bunch of fresh tire tracks in the dirt. Probably high school kids who had come up the past weekend to party, he assumed.

As they climbed the short hill to the pinnacle, Mick thought he saw movement ahead. As he got closer, he realized he saw two Harleys parked in front of the remnants of the old general store. WTF? It had to be the Kanes. They had gotten there early, too. No doubt to scout the area. Had they found Cassidy? He shuddered at the thought.

Mick figured Johnny realized the same time he did.

They pulled up next to the Kanes' Harleys and shut their bikes off. As Mick dismounted, Earl Kane appeared, holding a handgun on him. Travis came out from behind another burnt-out building, holding a pistol on Johnny.

"Whoa. Whoa," said Mick. "It's just us. No need for that." He made a gesture like "lower your guns" to Earl. Thankfully, Earl saw sense and put his pistol away.

"You come alone?" asked Earl.

"Yes. It's just us, like we agreed," said Mick, trying to reassure the Kanes. Mick noticed that Travis was in the process of tucking his gun into his waistband, too.

"So I got Lyle's map," said Mick, tapping his pocket. "I had to ride into Phoenix yesterday to retrieve it."

"Yes. We know," said Travis.

As Mick had suspected, someone had been watching them.

"So before we go get Lyle's secret stash for ya, I just have one question."

"What's that?" asked Travis Kane.

"Why did you kill poor Lyle? You could have just beaten him up."

"He owed our bosses money. We did what had to be done," smiled Earl Kane. "We needed to send a message."

"Fair enough," shrugged Johnny with his hands still in the air. "Message received."

"Okay, quit stalling. Where is the stash buried?" asked Earl.

Mick made a big show of pulling out the sketch Cass had drawn up the afternoon before of the landmarks in Dead Coyote Canyon. He unfolded the makeshift map and pretended to study it.

"This way," said Mick, pointing towards some busted-up railway tracks.

Travis Kane, Johnny, and Mick started to walk towards the tracks. Earl hung back before dipping behind the remnants of an old building.

Mick turned to see what was going on. It was at that moment that he heard a yelp.

Cassidy?

Earl reappeared with Cass in a headlock and his pistol by her head.

"You stupid fucks. You think you could get one over on us?" snarled Earl Kane.

He grabbed Cass's cell phone from her, the one she had secretly recorded Earl's confession on, and tossed it into the brush.

"Shit," swore Mick under his breath. We are screwed.

No weapons. A gun to Cassidy's head and no hidden secret stash of Earl's money to appease the Kane brothers. Mick figured they were toast. He had only moments to think of a plan to save their skins. The trouble was he couldn't think of anything.

"Gimme that map," said Travis Kane to Mick. Still shocked that the Kane brothers had found Cassidy and trashed her cell phone, he numbly passed over the map to the younger Kane.

In his mind, he saw how this was going to play out. They would dig where Lyle's "buried treasure" was supposed to be. They would find nothing. They would kill Cassidy, Johnny, and him out of spite, and that would be that. Mick had been in many near-death situations in his adult life, but this was one he could see no way out of.

Travis Kane examined the map.

"Over here," he instructed everyone.

He reached a spot that was between a bit of busted-up railroad track and some bushes.

"I think it's here," he said, looking at Earl Kane.

Travis shrugged off his backpack and flung it to the ground. Keeping his distance from both Mick and Johnny, he opened the pack and retrieved two folding shovels.

"Here, start digging," he said, kicking the dirt with his boot.

Mick tried to hide his nervousness. If he dug too slowly, the Kanes would get suspicious. If he dug too fast, they would realize they had been played the fool, and Johnny, Cassidy, and he would be having a dirt nap. He was torn.

The folding shovels were not full-size; he and Johnny had to kneel to dig. Mick hated that, as being on your knees made them a lot easier to kill if the Kanes got frustrated.

The dirt was actually easier to dig than expected. Fairly loose and not as compacted as Mick expected it to be.

Earl and Travis stood over Johnny and Mick as they dug. Mick noticed that Earl still had a grip on poor Cassidy and that he still had his pistol pointed in her direction.

He thought about cracking a few jokes to get them laughing and off guard. But that could backfire on them, so he chose to remain silent.

They kept digging. They were now a good foot and a half down. How much longer could they keep up this charade before the Kanes realized they were being played?

They kept digging. Then it happened. A telltale clunk. They had hit something.

"Wait, wait. What was that?" asked Earl Kane, peering into the hole.

"I think we found it," said Johnny, as surprised as Mick.

"Keep going," said Travis Kane, urging them on.

They kept digging. Mick could see what appeared to be an old military ammo can. What were the odds?

He and Johnny started clearing dirt away from the sides of the ammo can. There was now enough room for someone to get a good grip on it.

"Alright. Alright, back it up," said Earl. He slipped his semiautomatic pistol into his waistband.

Johnny and Mick backed away from the hole. Mick contemplated trying to make a run for it, but they would probably make it about ten feet before one of the wretched Kanes put a bullet into one of them. He could do nothing but leave his life in fate's hands.

Travis Kane leaned in and helped his brother pull the steel ammo can out of the dirt. Finally, it came free.

This was probably it, figured Mick. The can would be empty, and the Kanes would unleash their fury on the three of them.

"What have we got, bro?" asked Travis Kane, greedily staring at the ammo can.

"Hold on, Trav, let me find out," Earl replied.

The older Kane struggled to pop the lock on the can. Mick figured it had probably been buried for some time and had been rusted shut, but who knows?

Earl Kane finally got the lid unlocked, and that's when all hell broke loose.

Chapter 15 – Truth in Flames

Blue dye blasted into Earl Kane's face. Johnny was quicker to react than Mick. He realized right away that it was his chance and launched himself at Travis Kane. Travis went down with Johnny raining a flurry of blows on the hapless murderer's face.

Mick sprang up and raced to Earl, who was still stunned from the blast of blue dye to the face. He kicked Earl in the head with full force. Earl screamed as he went down. Mick jumped on top of him, Hulk Hogan "leg drop of doom" style, knocking the wind out of the elder Kane brother.

At that moment, Mick heard shouting. Now what?

Then he realized it was law enforcement, yelling at everyone to put their hands in the air. What? How?

He rolled off Earl Kane and raised his hands. The last thing he wanted was some trigger-happy cop blasting him full of bullets after surviving his run-in with the Kanes.

Two sheriff's deputies came running up and put the Kane brothers in cuffs.

"We are innocent!" shouted Johnny.

The sheriff swaggered up with a smile on his face.

"Yeah, I know. Cass already told me," said the sheriff.

Cass? Cass had called the cops? When? Thought Mick.

"You okay, lil sis?" asked the sheriff.

"Yeah, I'm fine. Thanks, big brother," smiled Cassidy, dusting dirt off herself.

"What the hell?" asked Mick.

"Cass called me last night and explained the situation," smiled the sheriff. "We have been out here since 5 am."

"Oh shit," said Johnny.

"We have their entire confession on tape thanks to you guys," said the sheriff.

"But Cassidy's cell phone?" said Johnny.

"Oh yeah! My phone," said Cassidy, running off to go find it.

"Don't worry. We have two different angles on the whole thing," said Sheriff Lane. "In case you haven't figured it out yet, it was us who planted the ammo can with the dye pack in it."

"Nice move," said Mick. As a rule, he had always lived his life with as little interaction with law enforcement as possible. This was one of the few times he was glad to see the boys in blue.

Chapter 16 – The Dust Settles

Mick and Johnny hung back as the sheriffs took the Kane brothers to jail. Cassidy had ridden up with her brother but elected to ride back with Mick and Johnny.

"Wow, I never knew your brother was the local sheriff," said Mick.

"You never asked," smiled Cass.

"True. When did you call him?"

"Last night, after you guys left. He was the one who lent me the dye pack, plus he suggested burying the ammo can there. He figured the Kane brothers would try to show up early and pull a fast one on you both."

"Yeah. We would have been screwed if you hadn't gotten him involved," quipped Johnny. "So thanks for that."

"Of course. I couldn't let my favorite two bikers get hurt. Could I?" laughed Cassidy.

"Aw shucks," joked Johnny.

"So what now?" asked Mick.

"I don't know about you, but I need some peace and quiet after all this excitement," said Cass.

"Okay…"

"So how about one of you gentlemen give me a ride back to town?"

Mick and Johnny looked at each other, mentally deciding who would give Cass a ride back to her bar.

"And then once we are back in town, let me pack a bag so I can finally witness this big stunt show of yours."

Johnny and Mick looked ecstatic. They had gotten used to having Cass around in the last few days.

"Well, we have missed the Scottsdale show," said Mick, "but we have a big show in Pomona, California, this coming weekend, if that works for you."

"Love California. I'm down," said Cass.

"We are going to have to return to Flagstaff and get our RV, though," said Mick.

"That's fine. I can wait," said Cass.

"Well, in that case, let's get moving," said Johnny.

Chapter 17 – The Road Ahead

With their names cleared, Mick and Johnny hit the open road once more, Cass traveling with them. They know freedom will always be fleeting, but the brotherhood, and now Cass, make the journey worth it.

Blood Debt

The desert wind carried the smell of oil and dust as Jesse "Crow" Mallory pulled his Harley into the gravel lot of the Ridge Runner Saloon. The sun was low, bleeding out over the Arizona hills, casting everything in that burnt orange glow his father used to call "the color of sin."

Inside, the place was half-empty. A jukebox whispered Merle Haggard, and the few patrons who were there didn't look up. But one man did. A thick-necked biker with a faded Iron Dogs MC patch on his cut. The same patch Jesse had seen the night his father was gunned down behind a roadhouse outside Tucson.

Jesse's heart thudded. His hand slid to the revolver under his jacket.

"Evenin', kid," the Dog said, voice rough as gravel. "You lost?"

Jesse shook his head slowly. "No. Just settling an old score."

The Dog chuckled, draining his beer. "You, Mallory's boy?"

Jesse nodded once. That was all the answer needed.

The man stood, wiping his mouth with the back of his hand, a cruel grin spreading. "Then I guess we both know how this ends."

It ended in three gunshots.

One for his father.

Two to make sure.

When the smoke cleared, Jesse holstered his pistol, heart hammering, and walked out into the dying light.

By the time he hit the state line that night, the word was already out. The Iron Dogs wanted his head, alive or dead; it didn't matter. Every gas station, bar, and biker dive from Yuma to Flagstaff would soon know his name.

Jesse gunned the throttle, his bike roaring down the highway like a demon set loose. He didn't look back, though he knew they'd be coming, patched-up hounds sniffing for blood, carrying vengeance like a torch.

He thought of his old man, Big Ray Mallory, founder of the Desert Sons MC, and the code he used to preach: "You spill blood, you pay in blood. But you never run from your name."

Jesse didn't plan on running. Not forever.

He'd hole up in the ghost towns, ride the backroads where the law and the Dogs didn't tread, gather his brothers, those still loyal to the Sons, and when the time came, he'd ride straight into the lion's den.

Until then, he kept his pistol close, his motor louder than his heartbeat, and the memory of his father alive in the rumble beneath him.

The price on his head was just the beginning.

Because Jesse Mallory wasn't done paying blood debts.

Thank You!

Hey this is Alex. If you have made it this far, Thank you!

I had a lot of fun writing this collection of short stories and I wanted to thank you for reading it.

If you enjoyed Fuel, Fire and Freedom: A Collection of Outlaw Biker Tales please consider leaving a review on Amazon as that would greatly help me out.

Please also check out my novel: Broken Brotherhood – An Outlaw Biker Tale

https://www.amazon.com/Broken-Brotherhood-Outlaw-BikerTale-ebook/dp/B0F2LMNBHD

I've a ton of stories in the pipeline if you want to keep updated on new books head on over to my website : www.alexmcrae.net.

Also feel free to follow me on Amazon here: https://www.amazon.com/stores/AlexMcRae/author/B0F344WTHB

All for now

Alex

Arizona 2025

Extra special thanks to the following people:

Mooch, The Motorcycle Prophet, George Christie Jr, James 2, Hugo Dias and Jeremy Rogers.

www.ingramcontent.com/pod-product-compliance
Lightning Source LLC
Chambersburg PA
CBHW032121170626
46808CB00006B/2053